Rachel caught his arm.

Seth turned back to her, his gaze first settling where her fingers circled his rain-slick forearm, then rising to meet hers. His eyes were forest-green in the low light, as deep and mysterious as the rainy woods outside the car.

"You saved my life last night, and you've asked for nothing in return. You didn't even try to use it against me just now, when you could have. Any con man worth his salt would have."

He grimaced. "I'm no saint."

"I'm not saying you are. I'm just saying I believe you."

The interior of the car seemed to contract, the space between their bodies suddenly infinitesimal. She could feel heat radiating from his body, answered by her own. Despite his battered condition, despite the million and one reasons she shouldn't feel this aching magnetism toward him, she couldn't pretend she didn't find him attractive.

PAULA GRAVES

THE SMOKY MOUNTAIN MIST

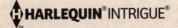

HARLEQUIN® INTRIGUE®

For the old Lakewood gang, those still with us and those gone, who made trips to the Smokies so much fun.

Recycling programs for this product may not exist in your area.

ISBN-13: 978-0-373-69699-4

THE SMOKY MOUNTAIN MIST

Copyright © 2013 by Paula Graves

This is a work of fiction. Names, characters, places and incidents are either the product of the author's imagination or are used fictitiously, and any resemblance to actual persons, living or dead, business establishments, events or locales is entirely coincidental.

This edition published by arrangement with Harlequin Books S.A.

For questions and comments about the quality of this book, please contact us at CustomerService@Harlequin.com.

HARLEQUIN®
www.Harlequin.com

Printed in U.S.A.

ABOUT THE AUTHOR

Alabama native Paula Graves wrote her first book, a mystery starring herself and her neighborhood friends, at the age of six. A voracious reader, Paula loves books that pair tantalizing mystery with compelling romance. When she's not reading or writing, she works as a creative director for a Birmingham advertising agency and spends time with her family and friends. She is a member of Southern Magic Romance Writers, Heart of Dixie Romance Writers and Romance Writers of America.

Paula invites readers to visit her website, www.paulagraves.com.

Books by Paula Graves

CAST OF CHARACTERS

Rachel Davenport—For weeks, the people around her were targeted for murder. Now she's in a killer's crosshairs. But why? Does it have something to do with the trucking company she inherited after her father's death?

Seth Hammond—The former con man turned mechanic has changed his ways, but it's hard to live down his past. After he saves Rachel from a near-catastrophe, can he convince her to trust his offer of protection?

Delilah Hammond—Seth's sister wants to believe her brother has changed. But she's been burned by his lies in the past. When he needs her support at a crucial moment, will she give him one last chance?

Davis Rogers—Rachel's college boyfriend came to town for her father's funeral, then disappeared after leaving Rachel a couple of cryptic phone messages. Could he be involved with the threats against her?

Paul Bailey—Rachel's stepbrother steps in to run Davenport Trucking temporarily while Rachel deals with the aftermath of her father's death. But does he have an ulterior motive for suddenly involving himself so deeply with the company?

Rafe Hunter—Rachel's uncle stands to inherit her shares of Davenport Trucking if something happens to her. He's the only family she has left, but could his obvious affection for her mask darker intentions?

Antoine Parsons—The Bitterwood P.D. detective hasn't forgotten Seth Hammond's bad-boy days, so when Seth keeps showing up at all his crime scenes, Antoine has trouble believing he isn't up to his old tricks.

Sutton Calhoun—Once Seth Hammond's best friend from childhood, the security agent no longer trusts his old friend. What will he do when troubling evidence against Seth falls into his hands?

Chapter One

Rachel Davenport knew she was being watched, and she hated it, though the gazes directed her way that cool October morning appeared kind and full of sympathy. Only a few of her fellow mourners knew the full truth about why she'd disappeared for almost a year after her mother's sudden death fifteen years ago, but that didn't change the self-consciousness descending over her like a pall.

She locked her spine and lifted her head, refusing to give anyone reason to doubt her strength. She'd survived so far and didn't intend to fall apart now. She wasn't going to give anyone a show.

"It's a lovely gathering, isn't it?" Diane, her father's wife of the past eight years, dabbed her eyes with a delicate lace-rimmed handkerchief. "So many people."

"Yes," Rachel agreed, feeling a stab of shame. She wasn't the only person who'd lost someone she loved. Diane might be flighty and benignly self-absorbed, but she'd made George Davenport's last days happy ones. He'd loved Diane dearly and indulged her happily, and she'd been nothing but a caring, cheerful and devoted wife in his dying days. Even if Rachel had resented the other woman in her father's life—and she hadn't—she would have loved Diane for giving her father joy for the past eight years.

"I sometimes forget that he touched so many lives. With me he was just Georgie. Not the businessman, you know? Just a sweet, sweet man who liked to garden and sing to me at night." Fresh tears trickled from Diane's eyes. She blotted them away with the handkerchief, saved from a streaky face by good waterproof mascara. She lifted her red-rimmed eyes to Rachel. "I'm going to miss the hell out of that man."

Rachel gave her a swift, fierce hug. "So am I."

The preacher took his place at the side of the casket and spoke the scripture verses her father had chosen, hopeful words from the book of Ephesians, her father's favorite. Rachel wanted to find comfort in them, but a shroud of loss seemed to smother her whole.

She couldn't remember ever feeling quite so alone. Her father had been her rock for as long as she could remember, and now he was gone. There was her uncle Rafe, of course, but he lived two hours away and spent much of his time on the road looking for new acts for his music hall.

And as much as she liked and appreciated Diane, they had too little in common to be true friends, much less family. Nor did she really consider her stepbrother, Diane's son, Paul, anything more than a casual friend, though they'd become closer since she'd quit her job with the Maryville Public Library to take over as office manager for her father's trucking company.

She sometimes wondered why her father hadn't ceded control of the business to Paul instead of her. He'd worked at Davenport Trucking for over a decade. Her father had met Diane through her son, not the other way around. He had been assistant operations manager for several years now and knew the business about as well as anyone else.

Far better than she did, even though she'd learned a lot in the past year.

She watched her stepbrother edge closer to the casket. As his lips began moving, as if he was speaking to the man encased in shiny oak and satin, a dark-clad figure a few yards behind him snagged Rachel's attention. He was lean and composed, dressed in a suit that fit him well enough but seemed completely at odds with his slightly spiky dark hair and feral looks. A pair of dark sunglasses obscured his eyes but not the belligerently square jaw and high cheekbones.

It was Seth Hammond, one of the mechanics from the trucking company. Other Davenport Trucking employees had attended the funeral, of course, so she wasn't sure why she was surprised to see Seth here. Except he'd never been close to her father, or to anyone else at the company for that matter. She'd always figured him for a loner.

As her gaze started to slide away from him, he lifted the glasses up on his head, and his eyes snapped up to meet hers.

A zapping sensation jolted through her chest, stopping her cold. His gaze locked with hers, daring her to look away. The air in her lungs froze, then burned until she forced it out in a deep, shaky sigh.

He looked away, and she felt as if someone had cut all the strings holding her upright. Her knees wobbled, and she gripped Diane's arm.

"What is it?" Diane asked softly.

Rachel closed her eyes for a moment to regain her sense of equilibrium, then looked up at the man again.

But he was gone.

"I DON'T KNOW. She looks okay, I guess." From his parking spot near the edge of the cemetery, Seth Hammond kept an eye on Rachel Davenport. The cemetery workers had lowered the oak casket into the gaping grave nearly twenty minutes ago, and most of the gathered mourners had dispersed, leaving the immediate family to say their final private goodbyes to George Davenport.

"It's not a coincidence that everyone around her is gone." The deep voice rumbling through the cell phone receiver like an annoying fly in Seth's ear belonged to Adam Brand, FBI special agent in charge. Seth had no idea why the D.C.-based federal agent was so interested in a trucking company heiress from the Smoky Mountains of Tennessee, but Brand paid well, and Seth wasn't in a position to say no to an honest job.

The only alternative was a dishonest job, and while he'd once been damned good at dishonesty, he'd found little satisfaction in those endeavors. It was a curse, he supposed, when the thing you could do the best was something that sucked the soul right out of you.

"I agree. It's not a coincidence." Seth's viewpoint from the car several yards away wasn't ideal, but the last thing a man with his reputation needed was to be spotted watching a woman through binoculars. So he had to make do with body language rather than facial expressions to get a sense of what Rachel Davenport was thinking and feeling. Grief, obviously. It covered her like morning fog in the Smokies, deceptively ephemeral. She stood straight, her chin high, her movements composed and measured. But he had a strong feeling that the slightest nudge would send her crumbling into ruins.

Everyone was gone now. Her mother by her own hand fifteen years ago, her father by cancer three days ago. No brothers or sisters, save for her stepbrother, Paul, and it wasn't like they'd grown up together as real siblings the way Seth and his sister had.

"Have you seen Delilah recently?" Brand asked with

his usual uncanny way of knowing the paths Seth's mind was traveling at any given moment.

"Ran into her at Ledbetter's Café over the weekend," Seth answered. He left it at that. He wasn't going to gossip about his sister.

Brand had never said, and Seth had never asked, why he didn't just call up Delilah himself if he wanted to know how she was doing. Seth assumed things had gone sideways between them at some point. Probably why Dee had left the FBI years ago and eventually gone to work for Cooper Security. At the time, Seth had felt relieved by his sister's choice, well aware of the risk that, sooner or later, his sister's job and his own less savory choice of occupations might collide.

Of course, now that he'd found his way onto the straight and narrow, she was having trouble believing in the new, improved Seth Hammond.

"I got some good snaps of the funeral-goers, I think. I'll check them out when I get a chance." A hard thud on the passenger window made him jerk. He looked up to find Delilah's sharp brown eyes burning holes into the glass window separating them. "Gotta go," he said to Brand and hung up, shoving the cell phone into his pocket. He slanted a quick look at the backseat to make sure he'd concealed the surveillance glasses he'd been using to take images of the funeral. They were safely hidden in his gym bag on the floorboard.

With a silent sigh, he lowered the passenger window. "Hey, Dee."

"What are you doin' here?" His sister had been back in Tennessee for two weeks and already she'd shed her citified accent for the hard Appalachian twang of her childhood. "Up to somethin'?"

Her suspicious tone poked at his defensive side. "I was attending my boss's funeral."

"Funeral's over, and yet here you are." Delilah looked over the top of the car toward the Davenport family. "You thinking of conning a poor, grieving heiress out of her daddy's money?"

"Funny."

"I'm serious as a heart attack." Her voice rose slightly, making him wince.

He glanced at the Davenport family, wondering if they had heard. "You're making a scene, Dee."

"Hammonds are good at making scenes, Seth. You know that." Delilah reached into the open window, unlatched the car door and pulled it open, sliding into the passenger seat. "Better?"

"You ran into Mama, did you?" he asked drily, not missing the bleak expression in her dark eyes.

"The Bitterwood P.D. called me to come pick her up or they were throwing her in the drunk tank." Delilah grimaced. "Who the hell told them I was back in town, anyway?"

"Sugar, there ain't no lyin' low in Bitterwood. Too damned small and too damned nosy." Unlike his sister, he'd never really left the hills, though he'd kept clear of Bitterwood for a few years to let the dust settle. If not for Cleve Calhoun's stroke five years ago, he might never have come back. But Cleve had needed him, and Seth had found a bittersweet sort of satisfaction in trying to live clean in the place where he'd first learned the taste of iniquity.

He sneaked a glance at George Davenport's grave. The family had dispersed, Paul Bailey and his mother, Diane, walking arm in arm toward Paul's car, while Rachel headed slowly across the cemetery toward another grave nearby. Marjorie Kenner's, if he remembered correctly. Mark Bramlett's last victim.

"I know vulnerable marks are your catnip," Delilah drawled, "but can't you let the girl have a few days of unmolested grief before you bilk her out of her millions?"

"You have such a high opinion of me," he murmured, dragging his gaze away from Rachel's stiffened spine.

"Well-earned, darlin'," she answered, just as quietly.

"I don't suppose it would do any good to tell you I don't do that sort of thing anymore?"

"Yeah, and Mama swore she'd drunk her last, too, as I was puttin' her ginned-up backside to bed." Bitter resignation edged her voice.

Oh, Dee, he thought. *People keep lettin' you down, don't they?*

"Tell me you're not up to something."

"I'm done with that life, Dee. I've been done with it a few years now."

Her wary but hopeful look made his heart hurt. "I left the truck over on the other side of the cemetery. Why don't you drive me over there?"

He spared one more glance at Rachel Davenport, wondering how much longer she'd be able to remain upright. Someone had been working overtime the past few weeks, making sure she'd come tumbling down sooner or later.

The question was, why?

"I DIDN'T GET to talk to you at the service."

Rachel's nervous system jolted at the sound of a familiar voice a few feet away. She turned from Marjorie's grave to look into a pair of concerned brown eyes.

Davis Rogers hadn't changed a bit since their breakup five years ago. With his clean-cut good looks and effortless poise, he'd always come across as a confident, successful lawyer, even when he was still in law school at the University of Virginia.

She'd been sucked in by that easy self-composure, such a contrast to her own lack of confidence. It had been so easy to bask in his reflected successes.

For a while at least.

Then she'd found her own feet and realized his all-encompassing influence over her life had become less a shelter and more a shackle.

Easy lesson to forget on a day like today, she thought, battered by the familiar urge to enclose herself in his arms and let him make the rest of the world go away. She straightened her spine and resisted the temptation. "I didn't realize you'd even heard about my father."

"It made the papers in Raleigh. I wanted to pay my respects and see how you were holding up." He brushed a piece of hair away from her face. "How *are* you holding up?"

"I'm fine." His touch left her feeling little more than mild comfort. "I'm sad," she added at his skeptical look. "And I'll be sad for a while. But I'm okay."

It wasn't a lie. She *was* going to be okay. Despite her crushing sense of grief, she felt confident she wasn't in danger of losing herself.

"Maybe what you need is to get out and get your mind off things." Davis cupped her elbow with his large hand. "The clerk at the bed-and-breakfast where I'm staying suggested a great bar near the university in Knoxville where we can listen to college bands and relive our misspent youth. What do you say, Rach? It'll be like Charlottesville all over again."

She grimaced. "I never really liked those bars, you know. I just went because you liked them."

His expression of surprise was almost comical. "You didn't?"

"I'm a Tennessee girl. I liked country music and bluegrass," she said with a smile.

He looked mildly horrified, but he managed to smile. "I'm sure we can find a honky-tonk in Knoxville."

"There's a little place here in Bitterwood we could go. They have a house bluegrass band and really good loaded potato skins." After the past few months of watching her father dying one painful inch at a time, maybe what she needed was to indulge herself. Get her mind off her losses, if only for a little while.

And why not go with Davis? She wasn't still in love with him, but she'd always liked and trusted him. It was safer than going alone. The man who'd killed four of her friends might be dead and gone, but the world was still full of danger. A woman alone had to be careful.

And she *was* alone, she knew, bleakness seeping into her momentary optimism.

So very alone.

For the first time in years, Seth Hammond had a place to himself. It wasn't much to talk about, a ramshackle bungalow halfway up Smoky Ridge, but for the next few weeks, he wouldn't have to share it with anyone else. The house's owner, Cleve Calhoun, was in Knoxville for therapy to help him regain some of the faculties he'd lost to a stroke five years ago.

By seven o'clock, Seth had decided that alone time wasn't all it was cracked up to be. Even if the satellite reception wasn't terrible, there wasn't much on TV worth watching these days. The Vols game wasn't until Saturday, and with the Braves out of play-off contention, there wasn't much point in watching baseball, either.

He'd already gone through the photos from the funeral he'd taken with his high-tech camera glasses, but as far as he could tell, there was nobody stalking Rachel Davenport at the funeral except himself. He supposed he could go through the photos one more time, but he'd seen enough of Rachel's grief for one day. He'd uploaded the images to the FTP site Adam Brand had given him. Maybe the FBI agent would have better luck than he had. Brand, after all, at least knew what it was he was looking for.

He certainly hadn't bothered to let Seth in on the secret.

You have turned into a dull old coot, Seth told himself, eyeing the frozen dinner he'd just pulled from Cleve's freezer with a look of dismay. *There was a time when you could've walked into any bar in Maryville and gone home with a beautiful woman. What the hell happened to you?*

The straight and narrow, he thought. He'd given up more than just the con game, it appeared.

"To hell with that." He shoved the frozen dinner back into the frost-lined freezer compartment. He was thirty-two years old, not sixty. Playing nursemaid to a crippled old man had, ironically, kept him lean and strong, since he'd had to haul Cleve Calhoun around like a baby. And while he wasn't going to win any beauty pageants, he'd never had trouble catching a woman's eye.

An image of Rachel Davenport's cool blue eyes meeting his that morning at the funeral punched him in the gut. He couldn't remember if she'd ever looked him in the eye before that moment.

Probably not. At the trucking company, he was more a part of the scenery than a person. A chair or a desk or one of the trucks he repaired, maybe. He'd become good at blending in. It had been his best asset as a con artist, enabling him to learn a mark's vulnerabilities without drawing attention to himself. Cleve had nicknamed him Chameleon because of his skill at becoming part of the background.

That same skill had served him well as a paid FBI informant, though there had been a few times, most recently in a dangerous backwoods enclave of meth dealers, when he'd come close to breaking cover.

But looking into Rachel Davenport's eyes that morning, he'd felt the full weight of being invisible. For a second, she'd seen him. Her blue eyes had widened and her soft pink lips had parted in surprise, as if she'd felt the same electric zing that had shot through his body when their gazes connected.

Maybe that was the longing driving him now, propelling him out of the shack and into Cleve's old red Charger in search of another connection. It was a night to stand out from the crowd, not blend in, and he knew just the honky-tonk to do it in.

The road into Bitterwood proper from the mountains was a winding series of switchbacks and straightaways called Old Purgatory Road. Back in the day, when they were just kids, Delilah, a couple of years older and eons wiser, had told Seth that it was named so because hell was located in a deep, dark cavern in the heart of Smoky Ridge, their mountain home, and the only way to get in or out was Purgatory Road.

Of course, later he'd learned that Purgatory was actually a town about ten miles to the northeast, and the road had once been the only road between there and Bitterwood, but Delilah's story had stuck with him anyway. Even now, there were times when he thought she'd been right all along. Hell *did* reside in the black heart of

Smoky Ridge, and it was all too easy for a person to find himself on a fast track there.

Purgatory Road flattened out as it crossed Vesper Road and wound gently through the valley, where Bitterwood's small, four-block downtown lay. There was little there of note—the two-story brick building that housed the town administrative offices, including the Bitterwood Police Department, a tiny postage stamp of a post office and a few old shops and boutiques that stubbornly resisted the destructive sands of time.

Bitterwood closed shop at five in the evening. Everything was dark and shuttered as Seth drove through. All the nighttime action happened in the outskirts. Bitterwood had years ago voted to allow liquor sales by the drink as well as package sales, hoping to keep up with the nearby tourist traps. While the tourist boom had bypassed the little mountain town despite the effort, the gin-guzzling horse was out of the barn, and the occasional attempts by civic-minded folks to rescind the liquor ordinances never garnered enough votes to pass.

Seth had never been much of a drinker himself. Cleve had taught him that lesson. A man who lived by his instincts couldn't afford to let anything impair them. Plus, he'd grown up dodging the blows of his mean, drug-addled father. And all liquor had done for his mother was dull the pain of her husband's abuse and leave her a shell of a woman long after the old bastard had blown himself up in a meth lab accident.

He'd never have gone to Smoky Joe's Saloon for the drinks anyway. They watered down the stuff too much, as much to limit the drunken brawls as to make an extra buck. But they had a great house band that played old-style Tennessee bluegrass, and some of the prettiest girls in the county went there for the music.

He saw the neon lights of Smoky Joe's ahead across Purgatory Bridge, the steel-and-concrete truss bridge spanning Bitterwood Creek, which meandered through a narrow gorge thirty feet below. The lights distracted him for only a second, but that was almost all it took. He slammed on the brakes as the darkened form of a car loomed in his headlights, dead ahead.

The Charger's brakes squealed but held, and the muscle car shuddered to a stop with inches to spare.

"Son of a bitch!" he growled as he found his breath again. Who the hell had parked a car in the middle of the bridge without even turning on emergency signals?

With a start, he recognized the vehicle, a silver Honda Accord. He'd seen Rachel Davenport drive that car in and out of the employee parking lot at Davenport Trucking every day for the past year.

His chest tightening with alarm, he put on his own emergency flashers and got out of the car, approaching the Honda with caution.

Out of the corner of his eye, he detected movement in the darkness. He whipped his gaze in that direction.

She stood atop the narrow steel railing, her small hands curled in the decorative lacework of the old truss bridge. She swayed a little, like a tree limb buffeted by the light breeze blowing through the girders. The air ruffled her skirt and fluttered her long hair.

"Ms. Davenport?" Seth's heart squeezed as one of her feet slid along the thin metal support and she sagged toward the thirty-foot drop below.

"Ms. Davenport is dead," she said in a faint, mournful tone. "Killed herself, you know."

Seth edged toward her, careful not to move too quickly for fear of spooking her. "Rachel, that girder's not real steady. Don't you want to come down here to the nice, solid ground?"

She laughed softly. "Solid. Solid." She said the word with comical gusto. "'She's solid.' What does that mean? It makes you sound stiff and heavy, doesn't it? Solid."

Okay, not suicidal, he decided as he took a couple more steps toward her. *Drunk?*

"Do you think I'm cursed?" There was none of her earlier amusement in that question.

"I don't think so, no." He was almost close enough to touch her. But he had to be careful. If he grabbed at her and missed, she could go over the side in a heartbeat.

"I think I am," she said. Her voice had taken on a definite slurring cadence. But he decided she didn't sound drunk so much as drugged. Had someone given her a sedative after the funeral? Maybe she'd had a bad reaction to it.

"I don't think you're cursed," Seth disagreed, easing his hand toward her in the dark. "I think you're tired and sad. And, you know, that's okay. It means you're human."

Her eyes glittered in the reflected light of the Charger's flashers. "I wish I were a bird," she said plaintively. "Then I could fly away over the mountains and never have to land again." She took a sudden turn outward, teetering atop the rail as if preparing to take flight. "She said I should fly."

Then, in heart-stopping slow motion, she began to fall forward, off the bridge.

Chapter Two

He wasn't going to reach her in time.

A nightmare played out in his head as he threw himself toward her. His hands clawing at the air where she'd been a split second earlier. His body slamming into the rail that stopped him just short of throwing himself after her over the side of the bridge. He could see her plummeting, her slender body dancing like a feather in the cold October breeze until it shattered on the rocks below.

Then his fingers met flesh; his arms snaked around her hips, anchoring her to him. Though she was tall and thin, she was heavy enough to fill the next few seconds of Seth's life with sheer terror as he struggled to keep her from tumbling into the gorge and taking him with her.

He finally brought her down to the ground and crushed her close, his heart pounding a thunderous rhythm in his ears. She pressed closer to him, her nose nuzzling against the side of his neck.

"This is nice," she said, her fingers playing over the muscles of his chest. "You smell nice."

His body's reaction was quick and fierce. He struggled to regain control, but she wasn't helping him a bit. Her exploring hands slid downward to rest against his hips. His heart gave a jolt as her mouth brushed over the tendon at the side of his neck, the tip of her tongue flicking against the flesh.

"Taste good, too."

He dragged her away, holding her at arm's length in a gentle but firm grip. "I need to get you home."

She smiled at him, but he could see in the dim light that her eyes were glassy. Clearly she had no idea where she was or maybe even who she was. Whatever chemical had driven her up on the girder was still in control.

"Rachel, do you have the key to your car?" He didn't want to leave her car there to be a hazard to other drivers trying to cross the bridge.

She shook her head drunkenly.

Keeping a grip on one of her arms, he crossed and checked the vehicle. The key was in the ignition. At least she hadn't locked the door, so he could move it off the bridge. But did he dare let Rachel go long enough to do so?

"Rachel, let's take a ride, okay?"

"'Kay." She got into the passenger seat willingly enough when he directed her there, and she was fumbling with the radio dials when he slid in behind the steering wheel. "Where's the music?"

"Just a minute, sugar." He started the car. A second later, hard-edged bluegrass poured through the CD speakers—Kasey Chambers and Shane Nicholson. He had that album in his own car.

She started singing along with no-holds gusto, her voice a raspy alto, and complained when he parked the car off the road and cut the engine.

"Just a minute and we'll make the music come back," he promised, keeping an eye on the road. There had been no traffic so far, but his luck wouldn't hold much longer.

He needed to get her out of there before anyone else saw the condition she was in.

He almost laughed at himself as he realized what he was thinking. He'd been a cover-up artist from way back, trying to hide the ugly face of his home life from the people around them. He'd gotten good at telling lies.

Then he'd gotten good at running cons.

Still, he thought it was smart to protect Rachel Davenport from prying eyes until she was in some sort of condition to defend herself. He didn't know what had happened to her tonight, or how big a part she'd played in her own troubles, but he didn't care. Everybody made mistakes, and she'd been under a hell of a lot more pressure than most folks these past few weeks.

She could sort things out with her conscience when she was sober. He wasn't going to add to her problems by parading her in front of other people.

He buckled her safely into the passenger seat of the Charger and slid behind the wheel, pulling the bluegrass CD from a holder attached to his sun visor. He put the CD in the player and punched the skip button until the song she'd been singing earlier came on. She picked up the tune happily, and he let her serenade him while he thought through what to do next.

Delivering her to her family was the most obvious answer, but Seth didn't like that idea. Someone had gone to deadly lengths in the past few weeks to rip away her emotional underpinnings, and Seth didn't know enough about her relationship with her stepmother and stepbrother to risk taking her home in this condition. She seemed friendly enough with them, but they didn't appear particularly close. In fact, there was some speculation at work whether Paul Bailey was annoyed at being bypassed as acting CEO. He might not have Rachel's best interests at heart.

The particulars of George Davenport's will had become an open secret around the office ever since he'd changed it shortly after his terminal liver cancer diagnosis a year ago. Everybody at the trucking company knew he'd specified that his daughter, Rachel, should be the company's CEO. It had been a bit of a scandal, since until that point in her life, Rachel Davenport had been happy working as a librarian in Maryville. What did she know about running a business?

She'd done okay, taking over more and more of her father's duties until his death, but would Paul Bailey have seen it that way?

The song ended, and the next cut on the album began, a plaintive ballad that Rachel didn't seem to know. She hummed along, swaying gently against the constraints of the seat belt. She was beginning to wind down, he noticed with a glance her way. Her eyes were starting to droop closed.

Maybe he should have taken her straight to the hospital in Maryville to get checked out, he realized. What if she'd overdosed on whatever she'd taken? What if she needed treatment?

He bypassed the turnoff that would take him to the Edgewood area, where Bitterwood's small but influential moneyed class lived, and headed instead to Vesper Road. Delilah was housesitting there for Ivy Hawkins, a girl they'd grown up with on Smoky Ridge.

A detective with the Bitterwood Police Department, Ivy was on administrative leave following a shooting that had left a hired killer dead and a whole lot of questions unanswered. Ivy had taken advantage of the enforced time off to visit with her mother, who'd recently moved to Birmingham, and had offered Delilah a place to stay while she was in town.

"Rachel, you still with me?" he asked with alarm as he noticed her head lolling to one side.

She didn't answer.

He drove faster than he should down twisty Vesper Road, hoping the deer, coyotes and black bears stayed in the woods where they belonged instead of straying into the path of his speeding car. He almost missed his turn and ended up whipping down Ivy Hawkins's driveway with an impressive clatter of gravel that brought Delilah out to confront him before he even had a chance to cut the engine.

"What the hell?" she asked as she circled around to the passenger door.

"You did some medic training at that fancy place you work, right?"

Delilah's eyebrows lifted at the sight of Rachel Davenport in the passenger seat. "What's wrong with her?"

"That's what I'd like to know." He gave Rachel's shoulder a light shake. She didn't respond.

"What are you doing with her?"

"It's a long story. I'll tell you about it inside." He nodded toward the door she'd left wide-open.

Inside the house, he laid Rachel on the sofa and pressed his fingers against her slender wrist. Her pulse was slow but steady. She seemed to be breathing steadily.

She was asleep.

He stood up and turned to look at his sister. She stared back at him, her hands on her hips and a look of suspicion, liberally tinged with fear, creasing her pretty face.

"What the hell happened? Did you do something to her?"

Anger churned in his gut, tempered only by the bitter

knowledge that Delilah had every reason to suspect him of doing something wrong. God knew she'd dug him out of a whole lot of holes of his own digging over the years until she'd finally tired of saving him from himself.

"I found her in this condition," he explained as he pulled a crocheted throw from the back of the sofa and covered Rachel with it. "On Purgatory Bridge."

"On the bridge?"

"*On* the bridge," he answered. "Up on the girders, about to practice her high-dive routine."

"My God. She was trying to kill herself?"

"No. She's on something. I thought maybe you could take a look, see if you could tell from her condition—"

"Not without a tox screen." Delilah crossed to the sofa and crouched beside Rachel. "How was she behaving when you found her?"

"Drunk, but I didn't really smell any liquor on her." The memory of her body, warm and soft against his, roared back with a vengeance. She'd smelled good, he remembered. Clean and sweet, as if she'd just stepped out of a bath. "She was out of it, though. I'm not sure she even knew who *she* was, much less who I was."

"Was she hallucinating?" Delilah checked Rachel's eyes.

"Not hallucinating exactly," Seth answered, leaning over his sister's shoulder.

She shot him a "back off" look, and he stepped away. "What, then, exactly?"

"She seemed really happy. As if she were having the time of her life."

"Standing on a girder over a thirty-foot drop?"

"Technically, she was swaying on a girder over a thirty-foot drop." Even the memory gave him a chill. "Scared the hell outta me."

"You should've taken her to a hospital."

Worry ate at his gut. "Should we call nine-one-one?"

Delilah sat back on her heels, her brow furrowed. "Her vitals look pretty good. I could call a doctor friend of mine back in Alabama and get his take on her condition."

"You have a theory," Seth said, reading his sister's body language.

"It could be gamma hydroxybutyrate—GHB."

Seth's chest tightened with dread. "The date rape drug?"

"Well, it's also a club drug—lower doses create a sense of euphoria. You said you found her near Smoky Joe's, right? She might have taken the GHB to get high."

He shook his head swiftly. "No. She wouldn't do that."

Delilah turned her head to look at him, her eyes narrowed. "And you would know this how?"

"We work in the same place. If she had any kind of track record with drugs, I'd have heard about it."

Delilah cocked her head. "Really. You think you know all there is to know about Rachel Davenport?"

He could tell from his sister's tone that he'd tweaked her suspicious side again. What would she think if he told her he was working for her old boss, Adam Brand?

As tempted as he was to know the answer, he looked back at Rachel. "If it's GHB, would it have made her climb up on a bridge and try to fly?"

"It might, if she's the fanciful sort. GHB loosens inhibitions."

Which might explain her drunken attempt at seduction in the middle of Purgatory Bridge, he thought. "How can we be sure?"

"A urine test might tell us," Delilah answered, rising to her feet and pulling her cell phone out of the pocket of her jeans. "But it's expensive to test for it, and it's almost impossible to detect after twenty-four hours." She shot her brother a pointed look. "Do you really want it on record that she's got an illegal drug in her system?"

Delilah might look soft and pretty, but she was sharper than a briar patch. "No, I don't," he conceded.

"We can't assume someone did this to her," she said, punching in a phone number. "After all, she just buried her father. That might make some folks want to forget the world for a while."

As she started speaking to the person on the other end of the call, Seth turned back to the sofa and crouched next to Rachel. She looked as if she was sleeping peacefully, her lips slightly parted and her features soft and relaxed. The calm expression on her face struck him hard as he realized he had never seen her that way, her features unlined with worry. The past year had been hell for her, watching her father slowly die in front of her while she struggled to learn the ropes of running his business.

He smoothed the hair away from her forehead. Most of the time when he'd seen her at the office, she had looked like a pillar of steel, stiff-spined and regal as she went about the trucking business. But every once in a while, when she didn't know anyone else was looking, she had shed the tough facade and revealed her vulnerability. At those times, she'd looked breakable, as if the slightest push would send her crumbling to pieces.

Had her father's death been the blow to finally shatter her?

Behind him, Delilah hung up the phone. "Eric says we just have to keep an eye on her vitals, make sure she's not going into shock or organ failure," she said tonelessly.

"Piece of cake," he murmured drily.

"We could take shifts," she suggested.

He shook his head. "Go on to bed. I'll watch after her."

He certainly wouldn't be getting any sleep until she was awake and back to her normal self again.

There was a long pause before Delilah spoke. "What's your angle here, Seth? Why do you give a damn what happens to her?"

"She's my boss," he said, his tone flippant.

"Tell me you're not planning to scam her in some way."

He slanted a look at his sister. "I'm not."

Once again, he saw contradictory emotions cross his sister's expressive face. Part hope, part fear. He tamped down frustration. He'd spent years losing the trust of the people who loved him. He couldn't expect them to trust him again just like that.

However much he might want it to be so.

BLACKNESS MELTED INTO featureless gray. Gray into misty blobs of shape and muted colors and, finally, as her eyes began to focus, the shapes firmed into solid forms. Windows with green muslin curtains blocking all but a few fragments of watery light. A tall, narrow chest of drawers standing against a nearby wall, a bowl-shaped torchiere lamp in the corner, currently dark. And across from her, sprawling loose-limbed in a low-slung armchair, sat Seth Hammond, his green eyes watching her.

She'd seen him at her father's funeral, she remembered, fresh grief hitting her with a sharp blow. She'd looked up and seen him watching her, felt an electric pulse of awareness that had caught her by surprise.

And then what? Why couldn't she remember what had happened next?

Her head felt thick and heavy as she tried to lift it. In her chest, her heart beat a frantic cadence of panic.

Where was this place? How had she gotten here?

Why couldn't she remember anything beyond her father's graveside funeral service?

She knew time must have passed. The light seeping into the small room was faint and rosy-hued, suggesting either sunrise or sunset. The funeral had taken place late in the morning.

How had she gotten here?

Why was *he* here?

"What is this?" she asked. Her voice sounded shaky, frightening her further. Why couldn't she muster the energy to move?

She needed to get out of here. She needed to go home, find something familiar and grounding, to purge herself of the panic rising like floodwaters in her brain.

"Shh." Seth spoke softly. "It's okay, Ms. Davenport. You're okay."

She pushed past her strange lethargy and sat up, her head swimming. "What did you do to me?"

His expression shifted, as if a hardened mask covered his features. "What can you remember?"

She shoved at the crocheted throw tangled around her legs. "That's not for me to answer!" she growled at him, flailing a little as the throw twisted itself further around her limbs, trapping her in place.

Seth unfolded himself slowly from the chair, rising to his full height. He wasn't the tallest man she'd ever met, but he was tall enough and imposing without much effort. It was those eyes, she thought. Sharp and focused, as if nothing could ever slip past him without notice. Full of mystery, as well, as if he knew things no one else did or possibly could.

Her fear shifted into something just as dangerous.

Fascination.

Snake and bird, she thought as he walked closer, his pace unhurried and deceptively unthreatening.

"What's the last thing you remember?" He plucked at the crocheted blanket until it slithered harmlessly away from her body. He never touched her once, but somehow she felt his hands on her anyway, strong and warm. A flush washed over her, heating her from deep inside until she thought she was going to spontaneously combust.

What the hell was wrong with her?

He asked you a question, the rational part of her brain reminded her. *Answer the question. Maybe he knows something you need to know.*

Instead, she tried to make a run for the door she spotted just beyond his broad shoulders. She made it a few steps before her wobbling legs gave out on her. She plunged forward, landing heavily against the man's body.

His arms whipped around her, holding her upright and pinning her against his hard, lean body. The faint scent of aftershave filled her brain with a fragment of a memory—strong arms, a gentle masculine murmur in her ear, the salty-sweet taste of flesh beneath her tongue—

She tore herself out of his grasp and stumbled sideways until she came up hard against the wall. Her hair spilled into her face, blinding her. She shook it away. "What did you do to me?"

She had meant the question to be strong. Confrontational. But to her ears, it sounded weak and plaintive, like a brokenhearted child coming face-to-face with a world gone mad.

Or maybe it's not the world that's gone mad, a mean little voice in the back of her head taunted.

Maybe it's you.

Chapter Three

Seth met Rachel Davenport's terrified gaze and felt sick. It didn't help that he knew he'd done nothing wrong. She clearly believed he had. And he would find few defenders if she made her accusation public.

Cleve Calhoun had always told him it never paid to help people. "They hate you for it."

What if Cleve was right?

"You're awake." The sound of Delilah's voice behind him, calm and emotionless, sent a jolt down his nervous system.

Rachel's attention shifted toward Delilah in confusion. "Who are you?"

"Delilah Hammond," Delilah answered. She took the crocheted throw Seth was still holding and started folding it as she walked past him toward the sofa. "How are you feeling?"

"I don't know," Rachel admitted. Her wary gaze shifted back and forth from Delilah to Seth. "I don't remember what happened."

Delilah slanted a quick look at Seth. "That's one of the symptoms."

"Symptoms of what?" Rachel asked, looking more and more panicky.

"GHB use," Delilah answered. "Apparently you did a little partying last night."

"What?" Rachel's panic elided straight into indignation. "What are you suggesting, that I did drugs or something?"

"Considering my brother found you about to do a double gainer off Purgatory Bridge—"

"I don't think you planned to jump off," Seth said quickly, shooting his sister a hard look. "But you were not entirely in control of yourself."

Delilah's eyebrows arched delicately. Rachel just looked at him as if he'd grown a second head.

"I was not on Purgatory Bridge last night," she said flatly. "I would never, ever…" She looked nauseated by the idea.

"You were on the bridge," he said quietly. "Apparently whatever you took last night has affected your memory."

"I don't…take drugs." Her anger faded again, and the fear returned, shining coldly in her blue eyes.

"Maybe someone gave something to you without your knowledge."

Seth's suggestion only made her look more afraid. "I don't remember going anywhere last night. I don't—" She stopped short, pressing her fingertips against her lips. "I don't remember anything."

"If you took GHB—"

Seth shot his sister a warning look.

She made a slight face at him and rephrased. "If someone slipped you GHB or something like it, it's not uncommon for you to experience amnesia about the hours before and after the dosage."

"What's the last thing you remember?" Seth asked.

Rachel stared at him. "I want to go home."

"Okay," he said. "I can take you home."

She shook her head quickly. "Her. She can take me."

Damn, that hurt more than he expected. "Okay. But what do you plan to tell your family?"

Her eyes narrowed. "Why?"

"I didn't know if you'd want people to ask uncomfortable questions."

Her expression shifted again, and her gaze rose to Seth's face. "My father would know what to do."

He nodded. "I'm sorry he's not here for you."

Her eyes darkened with pain. "Did you know my father asked if I thought he should hire you?" she said slowly. "He told me your record. Admitted it would be a risk. I don't know why he asked me. At the time, I didn't have much to do with the company. I guess now I know why."

"He trusted your instincts," Seth said.

She looked down at her hands. "Maybe he shouldn't have."

"What did you tell him?" Delilah asked, her tone curious. "About Seth?"

Rachel's gaze snapped up to meet Seth's. "I told him to give the man a second chance."

"Thank you," Seth said.

"I've been known to be wrong."

Ouch again.

Her eyes narrowed for a moment before she looked away, her profile cool and distant. To Delilah, she said, "I would appreciate a ride home. Do you think I should go to a doctor? To get tested for—" She stopped short, agony in her expression.

"Probably," Delilah said. "I could drive you to Knoxville if you don't want to see anyone local."

She shot Delilah a look of gratitude, the first positive

expression Seth had seen from her since she'd awoken. "Yes. Please."

As Delilah directed her out to the truck, she looked over her shoulder at her brother. "I'll take care of her." She followed Rachel out into the misty morning drizzle falling outside.

He nodded his gratitude and watched them from the open doorway until the truck disappeared around the bend, swallowed by the swirling fog. Then he grabbed his keys and headed out to the Charger, ignoring the urge to go back inside and catch some sleep.

He had to talk to a man about a girl.

No sign of recent sexual activity. The doctor's words continued ringing in her ears long after he'd left her to dress for departure. He'd said other things as well—preliminary tox screen was negative, but if she'd consumed GHB or another similar drug, it might not be easily detectible on a standard test. And depending on how long it had been since the drug was administered, it might not show up on a more specific analysis. He'd seemed indifferent to her decision not to test for it.

She supposed he had patients who needed him more than she did.

"How are you doing?" Delilah Hammond looked around the closed curtain, her expression neutral. There was an uncanny stillness about the other woman, an ability to remain calm and focused despite having a drug-addled woman dumped in her lap to take care of. She had a vague memory that there had been a Hammond girl from the Bitterwood area who'd become an FBI agent.

"I'm fine," Rachel lied. "Are you an FBI agent?"

Delilah's dark eyebrows lifted. "Um, not anymore. I

left the FBI years ago. I work for a private security company now."

"Oh."

"What did the doctor tell you?" she asked gently.

"No sign of sexual activity, but they also couldn't find a toxicological explanation for my memory loss. Something about the tests not being good at spotting GHB or drugs like it."

"You don't have any memory of where you might have gone last night?" Delilah picked up Rachel's discarded clothes from the chair next to the exam table and handed them to her.

"None. The last thing I remember is being at the cemetery."

Delilah left the exam area without being asked, giving Rachel a chance to change back into her own clothes in private. When Rachel called her name once she'd finished dressing, Delilah came back around the curtain.

"Look, I'm going to be straight with you," Delilah said. "Because I'd want someone to be straight with me. I know about Mark Bramlett and the murders. I know that they all seemed to be connected to Davenport Trucking in some way. Or, more accurately, connected to you."

Rachel put her fingertips against her throbbing temples. "Why do I feel as if everybody knows more about what's going on in my life than I do?"

"If someone's targeting you, up to this point it's been pretty oblique. But drugging you up and leaving you to fend for yourself outside on a cold October night while you're high as a kite?" Delilah shook her head. "That's awfully direct, if you ask me. You really need to figure out why someone would want you out of the way."

"You think I should go to the police."

The other woman's brow furrowed. "Normally, I'd say yes."

"But?"

"But is there any reason why it might not be in your best interest for the police to be involved?"

Rachel's head was pounding. "I don't know. I can't think."

"Okay, okay." Delilah laid her hands on Rachel's shoulders, her touch soothing. "You don't have to make that decision right now. Let's get you home and settled in. Is there someone there who can keep an eye on you until you're feeling more like yourself?"

"No," Rachel said, remembering that her stepmother had made plans to leave for Wilmington after the funeral. Diane's sister had invited Diane to visit for a few days. Paul had his own place, and while she and her stepbrother were friendly enough, she wouldn't feel comfortable asking him to play nursemaid. She already suspected he thought she was in over her head at the trucking company. He might even be right.

She didn't want to give him more reasons to doubt her.

"I'd offer to watch after you myself, but I have to drive to Alabama as soon as I can get away. I have a meeting with my boss, and it's a long drive. But you're welcome to stay at the house while I'm gone."

She wondered if Seth was staying there, too. She didn't let herself ask. "I'm okay. I'll be fine at home by myself."

"Are you sure?"

Rachel nodded, even though she wasn't sure about anything anymore.

"Smoky Joe" Breslin wasn't exactly thrilled when Seth roused him from bed on a rainy morning to answer a few questions, and his responses were laced liberally with profanities and lubricated by a few shots of good Tennessee whiskey. Seth had never been much of a drinker, so he nursed a single shot while Breslin knocked back three without blinking.

"Yeah, she was in here last night. Looked like a hothouse flower in a weed patch, but she seemed to be enjoying the music. And there were a few fellows who enjoyed lookin' at her, so who was I to judge?"

"Was she alone?" Seth asked.

"No, came in with some frat boy type. He tried a little something with her and she gave him a whack in the face, and some of the boys escorted him out. Not long after that, she headed out of here."

"What kind of condition was she in?"

"I don't know. I wasn't really watchin' when she left. I know she wasn't fallin'-down drunk or nothin'."

"You didn't check to make sure she wasn't driving?"

"Hell, you know how it can get around here on a busy night! I can't babysit everybody who comes here for the show. I do know she didn't have much to drink, so I didn't worry too much about it."

Which meant that unless she'd gone somewhere else to drink, it hadn't been alcohol alone that had put her up on that bridge.

"What can you tell me about the frat boy?" he asked Joe.

The older man grimaced. "Just some slicked-down city fellow. You know the type, comes in here with his nose in the air givin' everyone the stink-eye like he was better than them. I was glad to see the girl give him what for, if you want my opinion." Joe poured another glass of whiskey and motioned to top off Seth's.

Seth waved him off. "Did he pay for the drinks?"

"Yeah."

"Cash or credit?"

"Credit. One of them gold-type cards for big spenders. Flashed it like it was a Rolex watch or something."

"Would you have the receipt?"

Joe cut his eyes at Seth. "You pullin' another scam? I don't put up with that around here. You know that."

"No, no scam." He took no offense. "The woman he hit on is a friend of mine, see. I'd like to talk to the man about his behavior toward her."

"I see." Joe shot him an approving look. "Well, tell you the truth, she seemed to handle him pretty good all by her lonesome. But I'll see what I can dig up for you. Just promise me you're not gonna beat him up or shoot him or anything like that. I don't want the cops trackin' you back here and giving me any trouble."

"Just want to talk," Seth assured him, although if he found out that Frat Boy had anything to do with drugging Rachel Davenport, he couldn't promise he'd keep his fists to himself. She'd come way too close to going off the bridge the night before. She wouldn't have been likely to survive that fall.

Maybe the guy had slipped her something hoping it would make it easy to get lucky with her rather than to make her go off the deep end and hurt herself, but that distinction sure as hell didn't make drugging her any less heinous a crime.

And there was still the matter of the murders. Over the past two months, four women connected to Rachel Davenport had been murdered in what had initially seemed like random killings. Until investigators found the perpetrator and learned he'd been hired to kill those women and make the deaths look random. With his dying words, he'd admitted that it was "all about the girl."

All about Rachel Davenport.

Joe came back from the cluttered office just off the bar bearing a slip of paper. "Guy signed his name 'Davis Rogers.'"

The name wasn't familiar. Could have been someone Rachel knew from Maryville or even an old friend in town for her father's funeral. He'd ask her about him when she got back from the hospital.

The thought of her trip to Knoxville made his chest tighten as he left Smoky Joe's Saloon and headed toward the road to Maryville. He'd taken the past two days off work, but he was scheduled to work the next four. He had some vacation time coming to him, and he figured this might be the right time to take it.

He was surprised to find Paul Bailey in the office when he asked to see whoever was in charge while Rachel was out. Bailey had the account books open and looked up reluctantly when Seth stepped inside.

"Mr. Bailey, I've had a family situation come up. I know it's short notice, but I have a couple of weeks of vacation built up, and I'd like to take them now if possible."

Bailey's gaze was a little unfocused, as if his mind was still on whatever he'd been doing before Seth interrupted. "Yeah, sure. Nobody else has any days off scheduled, and they'll be happy to have the extra hours this time of year, with the holidays coming up. Just let Sharon at the front desk know what days you're taking, and she'll put it on the schedule."

"Thank you." Seth started to turn away, then paused. "I'm real sorry about Mr. Davenport."

"Thank you," Bailey answered with a regretful half smile.

On impulse, Seth added, "By the way, do you know a Davis Rogers?"

Bailey's gaze focused completely. "Why do you ask?"

"I just ran into a guy with that name last night at a bar," Seth lied. "He mentioned he knew the family. We drank a toast to Mr. Davenport."

"Last night?"

Seth kept his expression neutral. "Yeah. He mentioned he was thinking about selling his car, and I know someone in the market. I should've gotten his phone number, but I didn't think about it until afterward."

"He's not from here," Bailey said with a dismissive wave. "Probably couldn't work out a sale anyway before he heads back to Virginia."

Seth had a vague memory that Rachel had gone to college somewhere in Virginia. So, maybe an old college friend.

Maybe even an old boyfriend.

A sliver of dismay cut a path through the center of his chest. He tried to ignore it. "Thanks anyway." He left the office before Paul Bailey started to wonder why one of his fleet mechanics was suddenly asking a lot of nosy questions.

He stopped in the fleet garage, where he and the other mechanics shared a small break room. The three mechanics working in the garage today were out in the main room, so he had the place to himself.

Grabbing the phone book they kept in a desk drawer, he searched the hotel listings, bypassing the cheaper places. Joe Breslin had described Davis Rogers as a slicked-back frat boy, which suggested he'd stay at a nice hotel.

Was that Rachel's type? Preppy college boys with their trust funds and their country club golf games?

Drop it, Hammond. Not your concern.

She wasn't exactly what he considered his type, either. She was attractive, clearly, but quiet and reserved. And maybe if he hadn't begun to put clues together that suggested the recent Bitterwood murders were connected to Davenport Trucking, he might never have allowed himself to think about Rachel Davenport as a person and not just a company figurehead.

But ever since he'd given up the con game for the straight and narrow, he'd shown an alarming tendency to take other people's troubles to heart. And Rachel Davenport's life was eaten up with trouble these days.

An old twelve-step guy he knew had told him over-compensation was a common trait among people who felt the need to make amends for what they'd done. They tended to go overboard, wanting to save the whole damned world instead of fix the one or two things they could actually fix.

And here he was, proving the guy right.

Using his cell phone, he called Maryville hotels with no luck. He was about to start calling Knoxville hotels when he remembered there was a bed-and-breakfast in Bitterwood that offered the sort of services a guy like Davis Rogers would probably expect from his lodgings. The odds were better that he was staying in Knoxville, but Sequoyah House was a local call, so what would it hurt?

The proprietor at Sequoyah House put him right through to Davis Rogers's room when he asked. Nobody answered the phone, even after several rings, but Seth had the information he needed.

He had a few tough questions for Davis Rogers, and now he knew where to find him.

Chapter Four

On the ride back to Bitterwood, Rachel realized she had no idea where her car was parked. Seth had said he'd found her on Purgatory Bridge, so it made sense that she'd left her car somewhere in the area. Delilah agreed to detour to the bridge to take a look.

Sure enough, as soon as they neared the bridge, Delilah had spotted the Honda Accord parked off the road near the bridge entrance, just as Seth had said.

"Do you have your keys?" Delilah asked as she pulled the truck up next to Rachel's car.

"Yeah. I found them in my pocket." God, she wished she could erase the last twenty-four hours and start fresh. But then, she'd have to face her father's funeral all over again. Feel the pain of saying goodbye all over again. The stress of staying strong and not breaking. Not letting anyone see her crumble.

What would those mourners at the funeral have thought, she wondered, if they'd seen her acrobatics on the steel girders of Purgatory Bridge last night?

She shuddered at the thought, not just the idea of making a spectacle of herself in front of those people, but also the idea of Purgatory Bridge itself. Crossing the delicate-looking truss bridge in a car was nerve-racking enough. Standing on the railings with land a terrifying thirty feet below?

Unimaginable.

The morning rain had gone from a soft drizzle to sporadic showers. Currently it wasn't raining, but fog swirled around them like lowering clouds. As Rachel crunched her way across the wet gravel on the shoulder of the road, Delilah rolled down the passenger window. "You sure you feel up to driving?"

"I'm fine," she said automatically.

"Take care of yourself, okay?" Delilah smiled gently as she rolled the window back up, shutting out the damp coolness of the day. Rachel watched until the truck disappeared around the bend before she slid behind the wheel of the Honda.

The car's interior seemed oppressively silent, her sudden sense of isolation exacerbated by the tendrils of fog wrapping around the car. Outside, the world looked increasingly gray and alien, so she turned her attention to the car itself, hoping something would jog her missing memory.

What had she done the last time she was in her car? Why couldn't she remember anything between standing at her father's gravesite and waking up in a strange room with Seth Hammond watching her with those intense green eyes?

A trilling sound split the air, making her jump. She found the offending noisemaker—her cell phone, which lay on the passenger floorboard. Grinning sheepishly, she grabbed it and checked the display. She didn't recognize the number.

"Hello?"

"Rach! Thank God, I've been trying to reach you for hours."

"Davis?" The voice on the other end of the line belonged to her grad school boyfriend, Davis Rogers. She hadn't heard from him in years.

"I thought maybe you regretted giving me your number and were screening my calls. Did you get home okay?" Before she could answer, he continued, "Of course you did, or you wouldn't be answering the phone. Look, about last night—"

Suddenly, there was a thud on the other end of the line, and the connection went dead.

Rachel pulled the phone away from her face, startled. She looked at the display again. The number had a Virginia area code, but Davis had spoken as if he was here in Tennessee.

She tried calling the number on the display, but it went to voice mail.

He'd said he'd been trying to call her. She checked her own voice mail and discovered three messages, all from Davis. The first informed her where he was staying—the Sequoyah House, a bed-and-breakfast inn out near Cutter Horse Farm. She entered the information in her phone's notepad and checked the other messages.

In the last message, Davis sounded upset. "Rachel, it's Davis again. Look, I'm sorry about last night, but he seemed to think you might be receptive. I've really missed you. I didn't like leaving you in that place. Please call me back so I can apologize."

She stared at the phone. What place? Surely not Smoky Joe's. Why was her ex in town in the first place—for her father's funeral? Had she seen him yesterday?

And why had his call cut off?

SEQUOYAH HOUSE WAS a sprawling two-story farmhouse nestled in a clearing at the base of Copperhead Ridge.

Behind the house, the mountain loomed like a guardian over the rain-washed valley below. It was the kind of place that lent itself more to romantic getaways than lodgings for a man alone.

But maybe Davis Rogers hadn't planned to be alone for long.

Most of the lobby furnishings looked to be rustic antiques, the bounty of a rich and varied Smoky Mountain tradition of craftsmanship. But despite its hominess, Sequoyah House couldn't hide a definite air of money, and plenty of it.

The woman behind the large mahogany front desk smiled at him politely, her cool gray eyes taking in his cotton golf shirt, timeworn jeans and barbershop haircut. No doubt wondering if he could afford the hotel's rates.

"May I help you?" she asked in a neutral tone.

"I'm here to see one of your guests, Davis Rogers."

"Mr. Rogers is not in his room. May I give him a message?"

"Yes. Would you tell him Seth Hammond stopped by to see him about a matter concerning Rachel Davenport?"

He could tell by the flicker in her eyes that she recognized his name. His reputation preceded him.

"Where can he reach you?"

Seth pulled one of the business cards sitting in a silver holder on the desk. "May I?" At her nod of assent, he flipped the card over and wrote his cell phone number on the back.

The woman took the card. "I'll give him the message."

He walked slowly down the front porch steps and headed back to where he'd parked in a section of the clearing leveled off and covered with interlocked pavers to form a parking lot. Among the other cars parked there he spotted a shiny blue Mercedes with Virginia license plates.

Seth looked through the driver's window. The car's interior looked spotless, with nothing to identify the owner. If Ivy Hawkins weren't on administrative leave for another week, Seth might have risked calling her to see if she could run down the plate number. She'd investigated the murders that had started this whole mess, after all. She'd damned near fallen victim to the killer herself. She might be persuaded.

But her partner, Antoine Parsons, had no reason to listen to anything Seth had to say. And what would it matter, really? Seth already knew Davis was staying at Sequoyah House. Though if the car with the Virginia plates was his, it did raise the question—if he wasn't in his room, and he wasn't in his car, where exactly was he?

As he headed back toward the Charger through the cold rain, a ringing sound stopped him midstep. It seemed faint, as if it was coming from a small distance away, but he didn't see anyone around.

He followed the sound to a patch of dense oak leaf hydrangea bushes growing wild at the edge of the tree line. The cream-colored blossoms had started to fade with the onset of colder weather, but the leaves were thick enough to force Seth to crouch to locate the phone by the fourth ring. It lay faceup on the ground.

Seth picked up the phone and pressed the answer button. "Hello?" he said, expecting the voice on the other end to belong to the phone's owner, calling to locate his missing phone.

The last thing he expected was to hear Rachel Davenport's voice. "Davis?"

Seth's gaze slid across the parking lot to the car with the Virginia plates. His chest tightened.

"Davis?" Rachel repeated.

"It's not Davis," he answered slowly. "It's Seth Hammond."

She was silent for a moment. "This is the number Davis Rogers left on my cell phone. Where is he? What's going on?"

"I don't know. I heard the phone ringing and answered, figuring the owner might be looking for his phone."

"Where are you?"

"Outside Sequoyah House." He pushed to his feet and started moving slowly down the line of bushes, looking through the thick foliage for something he desperately hoped he wouldn't find.

"What are you doing there?" She couldn't keep the suspicion from her tone, and he couldn't exactly blame her.

"I went and talked to Joe Breslin at Smoky Joe's Saloon. He remembered seeing you there with a man last night. So he looked up the man's credit card receipt and got a name for me."

"I was at Smoky Joe's with Davis?" She sounded skeptical. "That is definitely not his kind of place."

"Maybe it's yours," he suggested, remembering her sing-along with the bluegrass CD.

"Did you talk to Davis?"

"The clerk said he wasn't in his room, so I left him a message to call me." He paused as he caught sight of something dark behind one of the bushes. "I used your name. Hope you don't mind." He hunkered down next to the bush and carefully pushed aside the leaves to see what lay behind.

His heart sank to his toes.

Curled up in the fetal position, covered in blood and

bruises, lay a man. Seth couldn't tell if he was breathing. "Rachel, I have to go. I'll call you back as soon as I can."

He disconnected the call and put the cell phone in his jacket pocket. The tightly packed underbrush forced him to crawl through the narrow spaces between the bushes to get back to where the man lay with his back against the trunk of a birch tree. He'd been beaten, and badly. His face was misshapen with broken bones, his eyes purple and swollen shut. Blood drenched the front of his shirt, making it hard to tell what color it had been originally. One of his legs lay at an unnatural angle, suggesting a break or a dislocation.

Seth touched the man's throat and found a faint pulse. He didn't know what Davis Rogers looked like, but the proximity of the battered man and the discarded cell phone suggested a connection. He backed out of the bushes, reaching into his pocket for his own cell phone to dial 911.

But before his fingers cleared his pocket, something hit him hard against the back of the neck, slamming him forward into the bushes. His forehead cracked against the trunk of the birch tree, the blow filling his vision with dozens of exploding, colorful spots.

A second blow caught him near the small of his back, over his left kidney, shooting fire through his side. That was a kick, he realized with the last vestige of sense remaining in his aching head.

Then a hard knock to the back of his head turned out the lights.

After ten minutes had passed without a call back from Seth, Rachel's worry level hit the stratosphere. There had been something in his tone when he'd rung off that had kept her stomach in knots ever since.

He'd sounded…grim. As if he'd just made a gruesome discovery.

Given the fact that he'd answered Davis's phone a few seconds earlier, Rachel wasn't sure she wanted to hear what he'd found.

What if something bad had happened to Davis? He'd been her first real boyfriend, the first man she'd ever slept with. The first man she'd ever loved, even if it had ultimately been a doomed sort of love.

She might not be in love with him anymore, but she still cared. And if Seth's tone of voice meant anything—

Forget waiting. She was tired of waiting. Seth had said he was at Sequoyah House. The bed-and-breakfast was five minutes away.

She grabbed her car keys and headed for the door. If she wanted to know what was going on, she could damned well find out for herself.

EVERYTHING ON SETH'S body seemed to hurt, but not enough to suggest he was on the verge of dying. He opened his eyes carefully and found himself gazing up into a rain-dark sky. He was drenched and cold, and his head felt as if he'd spent the past few hours banging it against a wall.

He lifted his legs one at a time and decided they were still in decent working order, though he felt a mild shooting pain in his side when he moved. Both arms appeared intact, though there was fresh blood on one arm. No sign of a cut beneath the red drops, so he guessed the blood had come from another part of his body.

He couldn't breathe through his nose. When he lifted his hand to his face, he learned why. Blood stained his fingers, and his nose felt sore to the touch. He forced himself to sit up, groaning softly at the effort, and looked around him.

He was in the woods, though there was a break in the trees to his right, revealing the corner of a large clapboard house. Sequoyah House, he thought, the memory accompanied by no small amount of pain.

Some of his memories seemed to be missing. He knew who he was. He knew what day it was, unless he'd been out longer than he thought. He knew what he'd been doing earlier that day—he'd been hoping to talk to Rachel Davenport's old friend Davis Rogers. But Rogers hadn't been in his room, so Seth had given the desk clerk a message for Rachel's friend and left the bed-and-breakfast.

He remembered walking back to the parking area where he'd left the Charger.

What then?

His cell phone rang, barely audible. He pulled it out from the back pocket of his sodden jeans and saw Adam Brand's name on the display. Perfect. Just perfect.

Then an image flashed through his aching head. A cell phone—but not this cell phone. Another one. He'd heard it ringing and come here into the woods to find it.

But where was the cell phone now?

He answered his phone to stop the noise. "Yeah?" The greeting came out surly. Seth didn't give a damn—surly was exactly how he felt.

"You were supposed to check in this morning," Brand said.

"Yeah, well, I was detained." He winced as he tried to push to his feet. "And the case has gone to hell in a handbasket, thanks for asking."

"What's happened?"

"Too much to tell you over the phone. I'll type you up a report. Okay?"

"Is something wrong? You sound like hell."

Seth spotted a rusty patch in the leaves nearby. His brow furrowed, sending a fresh ache through his brain. "I'll put that in the report, too." He hung up and crossed to the dark spot in the leaves.

The rain had washed away all but a few remnants of red. Seth picked up one of the stained leaves and took a closer look.

Blood. There was blood here on the ground. Was this where he'd been attacked?

No. Not him. There had been someone else. An image flitted through his pain-addled mind, moving so fast he almost didn't catch it.

But he saw enough. He saw the body of a man, curled into a ball, as if he'd passed out trying to protect his body from the blows. And passed out he had, because Seth had a sudden, distinct memory of checking the man's pulse and finding it barely there.

So where was the man now? Had whoever left this throbbing bump on the back of Seth's head taken the body away from here and dumped it elsewhere?

If so, they'd apparently taken the discarded cell phone, as well, because it was no longer in the pocket of his jacket.

He trudged through the rainy woods, heading for the clearing ahead. His vision kept shifting on him, making him stagger a little, and it was a relief to reach the Charger after what seemed like the longest fifty-yard walk of his life. He sagged against the side of the car, pressing his cheek against the cold metal frame of the chassis for a moment. It seemed to ease the pain in his skull, so he stood there awhile longer.

Only the sound of a vehicle approaching spurred him to move. He pushed away from the car and started to unlock to door when he realized the Charger was listing drastically to one side. Looking down, he saw why—both of the driver's-side tires were flat.

He groaned with dismay.

The vehicle turned off the road and into the parking lot. Seth forced his drooping gaze upward and was surprised to see Rachel Davenport staring back at him through the swishing windshield wipers of her car. She parked behind him and got out, her expression horrified.

"My God, what happened to you?"

He caught a glimpse of his reflection in the Charger's front window and winced at the sight. His nose was bloody and starting to bruise. An oozing scrape marred the skin over his left eye, as well.

"Should've seen the other guy," he said with a cocky grin, hoping to wipe that look of concern off her face. The last thing he could deal with in his weakened condition was a Rachel Davenport who felt sorry for him. He needed her angry and spitting fire so she'd go away and leave him to safely lick his wounds in private.

But she seemed unfazed by his show of bravado, moving forward with her hand outstretched.

Don't touch me, he willed, trying to duck away.

But she finally caught his chin in her hand and forced him to look at her. Her blue eyes searched his, and he found himself utterly incapable of shaking her off.

Her touch burned. Branded. He found himself struggling just to take another breath as her gaze swept over him, surveying his wounds with surprising calm for a woman who'd been swinging from the girders of Purgatory Bridge just the night before.

"Did you lose consciousness?" she asked.

"A few seconds." Maybe minutes. He couldn't be sure.

She looked skeptical. "Do you remember what happened?"

"I remember coming here to talk to your friend. He wasn't in his room."

"Right, but you found his cell phone."

He felt relieved to know his memory was real and not some injury-induced confabulation. "Right."

"But you cut me off. Said you had to go."

He caught her hand, pulling it gently from his chin and closing it between his own fingers. "Rachel, it's fuzzy, and I may be remembering things incorrectly—"

"Just say it," she pleaded.

He tightened his grip on her hand. "I think your friend Davis may have been murdered."

Chapter Five

The cold numbness that had settled in the center of Rachel's chest from the time she'd gotten Davis Rogers's call began spreading to her limbs at Seth's words. "Why do you think that?"

He told her.

She tugged her hand away from his and started walking toward the edge of the mist-shrouded woods. Seth followed, his gait unsteady.

"I can't prove any of it," he warned. "If you call the Bitterwood P.D., they won't believe a word of it. I'm not high on their list of reliable witnesses."

"I need to know for myself. Where was the blood?" Her feet slipped on wet leaves as she entered the woods.

Seth's hand closed around her elbow, helping her stay upright, despite the fact that he was swaying on his feet. "Over here." He nudged her over until they came to a stop near a large stand of wild hydrangea bushes. A fading patch of rusting red was trickling away in the rain, but it definitely looked like blood.

Rachel picked up one of the red-stained leaves and lifted it to her nose. A faint metallic odor rose from the stain. "It's definitely blood."

"I don't know what happened to him. I swear."

She turned to look at him. He really did look terrible,

blood still seeping from a scrape on the right side of his forehead and his nose crusted with more of the same. "You don't remember who did this to you?"

"No. Everything's a blur." He looked pale beneath his normally olive-toned skin. As he swayed toward her, she put out her hands to keep him from crashing into her.

"You're in no condition to drive."

He shot her a lopsided grin. "Neither is my car."

When they got back to the parking lot, she saw what he meant. Both of the driver's side tires were flat. She couldn't tell if they'd been punctured or if the air had just been let out of them. Didn't really matter, she supposed.

"Get in my car," she said, ignoring the wobble in her own legs. She didn't have time to fall apart. There was too much that needed to be done. She'd think about Davis later.

"Bossy. I like it." Seth shot her a look that was as hot as a southern summer. An answering quiver rippled through her belly, but she ignored it. He sounded woozy—probably didn't know what he was saying. And even if he did, neither of them was in any position to do much about it.

"I'm going to call the police and report Davis missing," she told him as she slid behind the wheel. "I'm going to have to include you in my statement."

He shook his head, then went stock-still, wincing. "Ow."

She turned to face him. He tried to do the same, but she could tell the movement was painful for him. Just how badly had he been beaten? "Seth, I can't leave you out of it, because you've left a trail that leads to you. You gave your name to the clerk. Your car is sitting here in the parking lot with flat tires, and if we call a wrecker to come get it, that's just another trail that leads to you."

His expression darkened. "You don't know what it's like to be everyone's number one suspect."

"You're right. I don't. But I can tell the police what I do know. I was talking to Davis when the line went dead. Then when I called Davis's phone, you answered—" She stopped short, realizing how that would sound to the police.

Seth's eyes met hers. "Exactly."

"If Davis is dead, I can't just do nothing."

"Just don't tell them I answered the phone."

He wanted her to lie to the police? "I can't leave something like that out of my statement."

He looked as if he wanted to argue, but finally he slumped against the seat. "Do what you have to."

She leaned back against her own seat, frustrated. What was she supposed to do now? Ignore his fears? Tell him he was overreacting?

She couldn't do that. Because she didn't plan on telling the police everything, did she? She certainly wasn't going to tell them she'd spent most of the previous evening apparently so drugged out of her head that she'd thought a balance beam routine on the girders of Purgatory Bridge was a good idea.

"I know what it's like to have people judging your every move," she said quietly.

He slanted a curious look her way.

"I don't want the police to know what happened to me last night. And you haven't pushed me at all to tell anyone the truth."

"I figured if you wanted it known, you'd tell it yourself."

She nodded. "I won't tell them you answered Davis's phone."

He released a long, slow breath. "Rachel, you know I didn't do anything to him. Right?"

She wondered if she was crazy to believe him. What did she know about him, really? He kept to himself at work, making few friends. She'd heard stories about his years as a con man, though she and her father had decided to judge him on his current work, not his checkered past. And he'd been a good worker, hadn't he? Showed up on time or early, did what he was asked, never caused any trouble.

But was that reason enough to trust what he said?

"I guess not." He reached for the door handle.

She caught his arm. He turned back to her, his gaze first settling where her fingers circled his rain-slick forearm, then rising to meet hers. In the low light, his eyes were as deep and mysterious as the rainy woods outside the car.

"You saved my life last night, and you've asked for nothing in return. You didn't even try to use it against me just now, when you could have. Any con man worth his salt would have."

He grimaced. "I'm no saint."

"I'm not saying you are. I'm just saying I believe you."

The interior of the car seemed to contract, the space between their bodies suddenly infinitesimal. She could feel heat radiating from his body, answered by her own. Despite his battered condition, despite the million and one reasons she shouldn't feel this aching magnetism toward him, she couldn't pretend she didn't find him attractive.

He wasn't movie-star handsome, especially now with his nose bloody and purple shadows starting to darken the skin beneath his eyes, but he was all man, raw masculinity in every angle of his body, every sinewy muscle and broad expanse.

He had big, strong hands, and even with a dozen conflicting and distracting thoughts flitting through her head at the moment, she could imagine the feel of them moving over her body in a slow, thorough seduction. The sensation was fierce and primal, intensely sexual, and she had never felt anything quite like it before.

"What now?" he asked, breaking the tense silence.

Her body's response came, quick and eager.

Take me home with you.

Aloud, she said, "I guess I call the police so they can start looking for Davis." She pulled out her phone and made the call to 911.

"I need to clean up," Seth murmured.

"Here." She reached across to the glove compartment, removed a package of wet wipes and handed them to him. "Best I can do."

He looked at the wet wipes and back at her, one eyebrow notching upward.

"Habit. I was a librarian," she said with a smile. "I dealt with a lot of sticky hands all day."

He pulled a wipe from the package and started cleaning off the blood, using the mirror on the sun visor to check his progress. When he finally snapped the wet wipe package closed, he looked almost normal. His nose wasn't as swollen as it had appeared with all the blood crusted on it, and the scrape on his forehead, once cleaned up, wasn't nearly as large as it had looked. Only the slight darkening of the skin around his eyes gave away his battered condition, and the rusty splotches where the blood from his face had dripped onto the front of his dark blue shirt.

"Better?" he asked.

She nodded. "You're going to have to answer questions regardless."

"I know." He slanted another wry grin in her direction, making her belly squirm. "I'd just like to look my best when I talk to the cops."

Uniformed officers arrived first to take their statements, but within half an hour, a detective arrived, a tall, slim black man with sharp brown eyes and a friendly demeanor. He'd come around the trucking company asking questions last month after a couple of their employees had been murdered, Rachel remembered. Antoine Parsons. Nice guy.

He didn't look particularly nice as his gaze swept the scene and locked, inevitably, on Seth's battered face. "Seth Hammond. You do have a funny way of showing up at all my crime scenes lately."

Seth's smile was close to a smirk. Rachel felt the urge to punch him in the shoulder and tell him to stop making things worse. But apparently he just couldn't help it. "Antoine, Antoine, Antoine. Still sucking up to the Man, I see. How's that working out for you?"

Antoine barely stopped an eye roll. "We have a missing person?"

Rachel stepped in front of Seth to address the detective. "His name is Davis Rogers. I was talking to him on the phone when I heard a thud and the phone went dead."

"You came here to look for him?"

"He'd left an earlier message on my voice mail, telling me where he was staying. It seemed the obvious place to look. I got here and found his car parked in the lot. But he's not in his room. And I found a patch of blood in the leaves nearby." She waved toward the woods.

Antoine's gaze slid back to Seth's face. "Who gave you a pounding, Hammond?"

"Not sure," he answered.

"What are you doing here? You with Ms. Davenport?"

"I came looking for Rogers. He wasn't in his room, so I was about to leave when I thought I saw something in the woods."

"Just happened to see something in the woods?" Antoine was clearly skeptical. Rachel was beginning to understand why Seth hadn't wanted her to include him in this police investigation at all. Maybe he'd earned the distrust, but clearly nobody in the Bitterwood Police Department was going to give him any benefit of the doubt.

"I heard something, actually." Seth slanted a look her way. She saw fear in his eyes but also rock-hard determination in the set of his jaw. "I heard a cell phone ringing. I found it on the ground beneath those bushes." He pointed toward the hydrangeas.

He was telling the truth about the phone, she realized with a thrill of surprise.

"It was Ms. Davenport, calling Rogers."

Antoine's brows lifted. "You said you were looking for Rogers. Why?"

She saw the hesitation in Seth's face. The truth, she realized, could be a scary thing. And not just for Seth. For her, too.

But it was better than the alternative.

She took a deep breath and answered the detective's question for Seth. "He was trying to find out what happened to me last night."

It took almost two hours to work through all the questions Antoine had for both of them. His attitude toward Seth had settled into guarded belief, though Seth knew it would last only as long as it took to get in trouble again.

At least Antoine had asked good, probing questions.

Unfortunately, neither Seth nor Rachel had any good answers. She still couldn't remember most of what had happened the night before, and Seth's memory of the attack that had left him bruised and half-conscious was similarly spotty.

He'd refused a trip to the hospital, though the paramedics thought he'd sustained a concussion. His mind was clearing nicely, and most of the aches and pains in his body had faded to bearable. He probably did have a mild concussion, but he didn't think it was any worse than that. He'd go spend the night at Delilah's and let her play nursemaid.

Except apparently Delilah was out of town for the night. "She said she was driving down to Alabama for a business meeting," Rachel told Seth after he'd assured the paramedics he'd have his sister keep an eye on him.

Well, hell. He'd just have to keep an eye on himself.

"You could stay with me tonight." Rachel's blue eyes locked with his, but her expression was impossible to read.

"That's kind of you—"

"I'm not sure it's kind," she said, the left corner of her mouth quirking upward. "I could use another set of eyes and ears in the house. I'm not inclined to stay there alone after all of this."

So when Antoine finally agreed to let them leave, Seth called a wrecker service to take the Charger to the local garage and got into the passenger seat of Rachel's car.

"You don't have to do this," he told her as she buckled herself in behind the steering wheel. "I'll be okay."

"I was serious. I don't want to be alone. I'm not sure I'm safe alone with everything that's going on."

She probably wasn't, he realized. "I'm sorry about Davis. I hope I'm wrong about what happened to him."

Her lips tightened. "I wish I believed you were."

"Do you know why he was here?"

"He must have come to the funeral." She looked close to collapse, he realized, so he didn't ask anything else until they reached the sprawling two-story farmhouse on the eastern edge of Bitterwood, a few miles south of Copperhead Ridge and light years away from the hard-scrabble life Seth had lived growing up on Smoky Ridge.

Until her father's cancer diagnosis, Rachel had kept her own apartment in Maryville, living off her earnings as a public librarian. But everything had changed when a series of doctors confirmed the initial diagnosis—inoperable, terminal liver cancer. Too late for a transplant to help. They'd given him four months to live. Chemo, radiation and a series of holistic treatments had prolonged his life by a few more months, but shortly before his death, George had said, "No more," and spent the remainder of his time on earth preparing his daughter to run the trucking company he'd built.

Seth knew all these intimate details about Rachel's life because Davenport Trucking was like any business that maintained a family atmosphere—everybody knew everybody else's business. Few secrets lasted long in such a place.

But he didn't know what Rachel thought about the drastic change in her life. Did she regret leaving the library behind? From what he knew of her work at Davenport, she had a deft hand with personnel management and seemed to have a natural affinity for the finance end of the business. People who'd grumbled about her selection as her father's successor had stopped complaining when it became clear that the company wouldn't suffer under her guidance.

But nobody seemed to know what Rachel herself

thought about the job. Did the benefit of fulfilling her father's dying wish outweigh the loss of a career she'd chosen for herself?

"This house is too big for just one person," Rachel commented as she unlocked the front door and let them inside. "I don't think Diane plans to come back here. Too much of my mother here for her tastes."

The front door opened into a narrow hallway that stretched all the way to a door in the back. Off the hallway, either archways or doors led into rooms on either side. To the immediate right, a set of stairs rose to the second floor, flanked by an oak banister polished smooth from years of wear. "Did you ever slide down that banister?" he asked Rachel.

"Maybe." A whisper of a smile touched her lips. "Think you can make it up the stairs? The bedrooms are on the second floor."

He dragged himself up the steps behind her, glad he was feeling less light-headed than he had back at the bed-and-breakfast. Rachel showed him into a simple, homey room on the left nearest the stairs. "I'll make up the bed for you. Why don't you go take a shower? The bathroom's the next door down on the right. There's a robe in the closet that should fit you. I'll see if Paul's left any clothes around you can borrow for the night."

When he emerged from the shower fifteen minutes later, he returned to the bedroom to find the bedcovers folded back and a pair of sweatpants and a mismatched T-shirt draped across the bed. A slip of paper lay on top of them. "Sorry, couldn't find any underwear. Or anything that matched. After I shower, we'll find something to eat."

She had finished her shower first and was already downstairs in the cozy country kitchen at the back of the house. "Something to eat" turned out to be tomato soup and grilled cheese sandwiches.

Rachel had finally shed the dress she'd worn to Smoky Joe's the night before, replacing it with a pair of slim-fitting yoga pants and a long-sleeved T-shirt that revealed her long legs and slender arms. She was thinner than Seth normally liked in a woman, but he couldn't find a damned thing wrong with the flare of her hips or the curve of her small, firm breasts.

"Is tomato soup okay? I should have asked—"

"It's fine. I can grill the sandwiches if you want."

She turned to look at him, smiling a little as she took in his mismatched clothes. Her stepbrother, Paul, was a little slimmer than he was, so the clothes fit snugly on his legs and shoulders. "Are you sure you're feeling up to it?"

"The shower worked wonders," he assured her, belly-ing up to the kitchen counter beside the stove, where she'd already prepared the sandwiches and set out a stick of butter for the griddle pan heating up over the closest eye. He dipped to get a better look at the stove top, relieved that it was a flat-top electric with no open-flame burners.

She gave him a sidelong glance as he moved closer to where she stood stirring the soup. "I'm not used to cook-ing with company."

"Me, either." He dropped a pat of butter on the griddle pan. It sizzled and snapped, and they both had to jump back to avoid the splatter.

Rachel laughed. "I see why. You're dangerous."

"We could switch," he suggested. "Surely I can man-age stirring soup."

Switching positions, they brushed intimately close. As Seth's body stirred to life, he realized the cut of the sweatpants wasn't quite loose enough to hide his reac-tion if he didn't get his libido under control, and soon.

Just stir the soup. Clockwise, clockwise, switch it up to counterclockwise—

"Why are you so interested in what happened to me last night?" Rachel broke the tense silence.

He glanced at her and found she was looking intently at the griddle, where she'd laid both of the sandwiches in a puddle of sizzling butter, her profile deceptively serene. Only the quick flutter of her pulse in her throat gave away her tension.

"What is it they say? Save a person's life and they're your slave forever after? Maybe I'm just waiting for you to pay up."

She cut her eyes at him as if to make sure he was teasing. "Yeah, that'll happen."

He grinned. "Maybe I'm sucking up to the new boss."

Wrong thing to say. Her slight smile faded immediately. "New boss. I haven't even let myself think about that yet."

"Is that going to be a problem? Me being an employee, I mean. And being here like this. Because I'm feeling a lot better, really. I don't have to stick around so you can watch out for my mental state."

"That's not what I meant," she said. "I was thinking about being the boss, period. All those people depending on what I do and say now."

He had stopped stirring while they were talking, and a thin skin was forming on top of the soup. He started stirring again, quickly whisking the film away. "Hasn't that been the case for a while now?"

She was quiet a moment. "I guess so. It just didn't feel real as long as my father was around to be my safety net."

To his dismay, he saw tears glisten in her eyes, threatening to spill. The urge to pull her into his arms and hold her close was almost more than he could resist. He settled for laying one hand on her shoulder and giving it a comforting squeeze.

She wiped her eyes with the heel of one hand and flipped the sandwiches over. "I had a long time to prepare for my father's death. And it was a relief by the end to see him finally out of pain. But now that I'm past that numb stage—"

"Your dad was a good man. Not many people would've taken a chance on someone like me. This world's a worse place with him gone."

His words had summoned tears again, but also a smile, which she turned on him like a ray of pure sunshine that brightened the room, even as the drizzle outside darkened the day.

He smiled back briefly, then forced his attention back to the soup before he got any deeper into trouble.

Chapter Six

After lunch, Rachel made a pot of coffee and they took their cups into the den on the eastern side of the house, where a large picture window offered a glimpse of Copperhead Ridge shrouded with mist. The rain had picked up again, casting the trees in hues of blue and gray. When she turned on the floor lamps that flanked the room, the scene outside faded into reflections of the warm, comfortably furnished den and the two slightly bedraggled people who occupied it.

Seth found his own reflection depressing, given how quickly his bruises were darkening, making him look like the loser of a cage match. He turned his attention instead to Rachel, whose honey-brown hair lay in damp waves around her face. Scrubbed clean and pink, she looked about a decade younger and prettier than she had any right to be.

"How's your head feeling?" she asked.

Light, he thought. But it didn't have much to do with his mild concussion. "Better. Not really hurting anymore."

Her brief smile faded quickly. "I don't know what to think about Davis."

"You mean whether or not he's still alive?"

She sank into an armchair across from the sofa, curling her legs under her. She waved for Seth to sit across from her on the sofa. "I mean if he's dead. How am I supposed to feel about it?"

"I don't know that you're *supposed* to feel any particular way," Seth offered. "You just feel what you feel."

"I did love him once. He was the first man—" She stopped short, a delicate blush rising in her cheeks. She slanted a quick look at Seth. "It didn't last. We wanted such different things out of life."

Whatever it had been that Davis Rogers had wanted out of life, it was surely closer to Rachel's desires than anything Seth had done or wanted to do in his own life. If she and Davis had been miles apart, she and Seth were separated by whole galaxies.

But it doesn't matter, does it? That's not why you're here.

"I haven't even seen him in years. We ran into each other a while back at a football game in Charlottesville. Said hi, promised to call but never did—" She closed her eyes. "Why did he come here?"

"Probably to attend your father's funeral and see how you were."

"And now he might be dead because of me."

Seth reached across the space between them, covering her hands with one of his. "If he's dead, it's because someone beat the hell out of him."

"Because of me."

He crouched in front of her, closing his fingers around her wrists. "Look at me."

Her troubled blue eyes met his.

"I know someone's been methodically removing people from your life to isolate you. I know whoever's pulling the strings hired Mark Bramlett to kill four women who were close to you. And now, maybe, he's killed your old boyfriend, who came to town to make sure you were okay. I think he may have been behind drugging you last night, too."

Rachel's eyes darkened with suspicion. "How do you know this?"

"I started to suspect something was going on when I realized three of the four Bitterwood murders involved women who'd worked at Davenport Trucking. That was strange enough. Then I asked around and found out that Marjorie Kenner had been your friend and mentor—another librarian, right?"

"Right." She looked stricken by his words, as if the mere reminders of all she'd lost had hit her all over again. He wished he'd found some way to soften his words, but he doubted anything he could have said would have made her feel the pain any less keenly.

"What I don't know," he added more gently, "is why. If someone wanted to get you out of his way—"

"His?"

"His, her—whichever. If someone wanted you out of the way, why not just kill you?"

She blanched. "I don't know."

"I think you do. You just can't say it out loud for some reason."

She slanted a troubled look at him. "How do you know so much about me?"

He ran his thumb lightly over her knuckles, gentling her with the movement. He saw her start to relax a little, soothed by the repetitive movement of his thumb. "I know because I observe. I used to be a con man, you know. That's what con men do. Observe, compile, formulate and exploit."

Her nostrils flared with a hint of distaste. "You're approaching my trouble like you would approach a potential mark?"

"Might as well use those skills for good."

Her eyes narrowed a little, but she gave a slight nod. "So what have you observed?"

"You're scared of something. Not everyone can see it, because you hide it really well. But I see it, because that used to be my job. Finding a person's vulnerable spots and figuring out how to use them."

"But you haven't found out what it is."

"Not yet."

Her lips twisted in a mirthless smile. "And I'm supposed to spill what it is to you, make it easier?"

"I'm not the one trying to hurt you."

"How do I know that?" She pulled her hands free of his grip and pushed him out of her way, rising and pacing the hardwood floor until she reached the picture window. She met his gaze in the window reflection. "I don't really know you. And what I do know scares me."

He couldn't blame her. What he knew about himself would scare anyone. "I don't want to see you get hurt, and whether you like my skill set or not, I can use it to help you out. So whatever you can tell me, whatever you're comfortable sharing—I'll listen. I'll keep your confidence, and I won't use it against you."

She turned around to look at him. "I'm taking a huge risk just letting you stay here, aren't I?"

She wasn't going to tell him what scared her so much, he realized. It was disappointing. Frustrating. But he didn't blame her.

"Okay." He nodded. "I can leave if you want me to."

She licked her lips and held his gaze, searching his expression as if trying to see what was going on inside his mind. "No. I know you're feeling better, but head injuries can be quirky. I'd rather you stay here where I can look in on you every few hours to make sure you haven't gone into a coma."

He grimaced. "What, you're planning to wake me up every couple of hours or something?" He added a touch of humor to his voice, hoping to lighten the mood.

It worked. Her lips quirked slightly, and there was a glitter of amusement in her blue eyes when she answered, "That's exactly what I'm planning to do."

Behind the humor, however, he heard a steely determination that caught him by surprise. She apparently took the job of keeping an eye on him seriously, and he suspected it was as much for her own sake as his. Maybe it gave her a welcome distraction from the strain and grief of her life these days.

He nodded toward the picture window. "Do you always leave these windows open like this?"

Her brow furrowed. "Most of the time. It's such a beautiful view."

"It is," he agreed. "But it gives people a pretty good view of you, too."

Her eyes darkened, and she wrapped her arms around herself as if she felt a sudden chill. "I never thought about that."

She wouldn't have. She wasn't used to being a target, and Seth wished like hell she could continue living her life without precautions. But there was too much danger out there, focused directly on her, for her to let her guard down that way anymore.

The windows were curtain-free, but he thought he saw levers on each double-paned window that suggested between-the-glass blinds. "Whenever it's dark enough outside to see your reflection in the windows, you should close the blinds."

She pressed her lips in a tight line, as if it annoyed her to have to make even that small accommodation to the dangerous world around her. A sign of a charmed life, he thought, remembering how early in his own life he'd learned to take precautions against the dangers always lurking, both outside and in.

Another way he and Rachel Davenport were worlds apart.

Starting at the opposite end of the room, he helped her close the blinds until they met in the middle. She paused at the last window, gazing out at the darkness barely visible beyond their reflections.

"You think I'm spoiled," she said quietly.

He didn't answer. He'd more or less been thinking exactly that, although not with any disapproval. He envied her, frankly.

"There's a lot about my life you don't know." She closed the blinds, shutting out the rainy afternoon, and turned to look at him, her expression softening. "You look terrible. I think you may have a broken nose."

It certainly hurt like hell, but he'd examined the bones himself while taking his shower, where he could throw out a stream of profanities without offending anyone. Cracked or not, the bones and cartilage were all in the right places. "It'll heal on its own."

"Said in the tone of a man who's had a broken bone or two."

"Or ten." He made a face. "I'm fine."

She looked skeptical but didn't press him on it. She crossed back to the armchair and curled up on its overstuffed cushions, pulling her knees up to her chest.

He didn't feel like sitting, so he wandered around the den, taking in the good furniture—some antiques, most not—and the eclectic collection of knickknacks dotting the flat surfaces around the large, airy room. Tiny animals sculpted from colored quartz formed a menagerie on a round side table near the sofa. On the fireplace mantel sat a small collection of Russian nesting dolls, painted in bright colors.

The fireplace itself was, thankfully, cold and unlit, though the extra heat might have helped to drive away the afternoon chill still shivering in his bones. He'd live without it, thank you very much.

He didn't care for fire.

The house he'd grown up in would have fit in this room, he thought, or close to it. He, Dee and his parents had lived there in grim strife for nearly fourteen years, until his father had blown the whole damned thing up, and himself with it.

He wondered what Rachel Davenport had been doing around the time of that explosion. Probably up to her eyeballs in homework from Brandywine Academy, the expensive private school she'd attended to keep her away from the Appalachian hillbillies who filled Bitterwood's public schools.

Envy is an unattractive trait. Cleve Calhoun's voice rumbled in his ear, full of wry humor. Hilarious advice coming from the man who'd used envy, greed, pride and vanity with great expertise against all his hapless marks. But however bad his motives for teaching Seth a few practical life lessons, Cleve had been right most of the time. Envy *was* an unattractive trait. And unfair to the envied, in Rachel's case.

It wasn't her fault she'd been loved and protected. Every child should be so blessed.

"Shouldn't you be resting?" Rachel asked.

He turned to look at her. "I'm not tired."

Her eyes narrowed slightly. "This isn't your first beating." It wasn't a question.

He didn't know whether to laugh or grimace. He managed something in between, his lips curving in a wry grin. "No, ma'am. It's not."

"Did you deserve them?"

That time, he did laugh. "Some of the time."

"Why did you choose the life you did?"

He wandered back over to the sofa, thinking about how to answer. When he'd been younger, he might have told her he didn't choose to become a con man. That life had chosen for him. He'd spent a lot of time blaming everyone in the world but himself for his troubles.

But everyone had choices, even people who didn't think they did. Delilah's childhood had been the same as his, but she'd chosen a different path, one that had made her a hero, not a criminal. He could have chosen such a path if he hadn't let hate and anger do him in.

That had been his choice. Nothing that happened before excused it.

"When I was young," he said finally, sitting on the sofa across from her, "I had a choice between two paths. One looked hard. The other looked easy. I chose easy."

A little furrow formed in her brow as she considered his words. "That simple?"

He nodded. "That simple. I was angry and tired of struggling. I was eaten up with envy and mad at the whole damned world. So when a man offered me a chance to get everything I wanted and stick it to people who stood in my way, I took it. I reckon you could even say I relished it. I was good at it, and in a twisted way, I think it gave me a sense of self-worth I'd never had before."

"So why aren't you still doing it?"

"Because nothing good, nothing real, gets built on lies."

Her solemn blue eyes held his gaze thoughtfully. "Or you could be lying to me now. Maybe this act of repentance is all for show."

"I guess that's for you to figure out."

She buried her face in her hands, rubbing her eyes with the heels of her hands. "I'm so tired."

He knew she wasn't just talking about physical tiredness. The past few months must have been hell on her emotionally, losing so many people who mattered to her, including her own father. "Why don't you go lie down? Take a nap."

"I'm supposed to be keeping an eye on you, remember?"

"I'm fine. Really. The ol' noggin's not even hurting anymore." *Well, not more than a slight ache,* he amended silently. And it was mostly at the site at the back of his head where he'd taken the knockout blow.

After a long, thoughtful pause, she rose to her feet with easy grace. He wondered idly if she'd taken ballet lessons as a child. She had the long limbs and elegant lines of a dancer.

Delilah had always wanted to take dance lessons, he remembered. He wondered if his sister had made up for lost time once she'd gotten away from Smoky Ridge. He'd have to remember to ask her.

"There's food in the fridge if you get hungry." She waved her arm toward the cases full of books that lined the walls of the den. "Lots to read, if your head's up to it. There's a television and a sound system in that cabinet if you'd rather watch TV or listen to music."

"In other words, make myself at home?"

Her lips quirked. "I'm not sure it's safe to give you that much rope."

He grinned back at her, unoffended. "Smart girl."

She headed for the stairs, but not before Seth saw her smile widen with pleasure.

RACHEL HADN'T PLANNED to take a nap. She had felt tired but not particularly sleepy when she'd climbed the stairs to her room on the second floor, but the whisper of rain against the windows and the long and stressful day colluded to lull her to sleep within minutes of settling on the chaise lounge in the corner of her bedroom.

When she next opened her eyes, the gloom outside had gone from gray to inky black, and the room was cold enough to give her a chill. She rose from the chaise, stretching her stiffened muscles, and started toward the bathroom when she heard it.

Music.

Seth must have taken her at her word and turned on the stereo system, she thought, surprised by his choice of music. She hadn't figured him for a Chopin fan.

Then she recognized the tune. Nocturne Opus 9, Number 2. It had been her mother's favorite.

It had been playing the night she'd died.

Rachel walked slowly toward the bedroom door, her gut tightening with dread. There were no Chopin CDs in the house. What the police hadn't taken as evidence, her father had gotten rid of shortly after her mother's death.

How had Seth found anything to play?

Did he know about how her mother had died? He might know the mode of her death, of course—the suicide had made the papers—but the gory details had never showed up in the news or even in small-town gossip. The police and the coroner had been scrupulously discreet, from everything her father had told her of the aftermath of her mother's death.

So how could he know about the music?

She pushed open the door. And stopped suddenly in the center of the hall as she realized the music wasn't coming from the den below.

It was coming from the attic above.

Acid fear bubbled in her throat, forcing her to swallow convulsively. Was she imagining the slow, plaintive strains of piano music floating down from above?

Was she reliving the night of her mother's death, the way she had relived it in a thousand nightmares?

She had heard music that night as well, swelling through the otherwise silent house. It had awakened her from a dead sleep, loud enough to rip through the fabric of her tearstained dreams.

She'd felt nothing but anger at the sound. Anger at her mother's harsh words, at the stubborn refusal to see things her way. She'd been fifteen and pushing against the fences of her childhood. Her father had been the more reasonable of her parents, in her eyes at least. He'd recognized her need to unfurl her wings and fly now and then.

Her mother had just wanted her to stay in the safe nest she'd built for her only child.

A nest that was smothering her to death.

She'd hated the sound of that music, the piercing trills and the waltz cadence. She'd hated how loud it was, seeming to shake the walls and shatter her brain cells.

Or maybe that had just been how it had seemed afterward. After she'd climbed the ladder up to the attic and seen her mother swaying to the music, her gaze lifted toward the unseen heavens, one hand waving in rhythm and the other closed around the butt of George Davenport's Colt .45 pistol.

Terror stealing her breath, Rachel stared up at the ladder. The very thought of climbing into the attic was enough to make beads of sweat break out across her forehead and slither down her neck like liquid fear.

But she had to know. Not knowing was worse, somehow.

Biting her lip so hard she feared she'd made it bleed, Rachel reached up and pulled the cord that lowered the ladder to the attic. Music spilled out along with the ladder, louder than before. Not the rafter-rattling decibels of her memories but loud enough.

Swallowing hard, she started to climb the ladder, clinging to the wooden rungs as if her life depended on it.

She'd had no warning of what she'd find that night. There were things she'd gotten used to about her mother—her obsession with cleanliness, her moodiness, her occasional outbursts of anger—but none of those things had seemed more than the normal foibles of life.

Maybe her father had sheltered her from the worst of it. Or maybe it wasn't as bad when her father was around. But he'd gone on a business trip, one that had eventually led to his securing the capital to start his own trucking business after working in truck fleet sales for most of his adult life. He was due back that night, but he'd been gone for almost a week.

Maybe a week had been all it had taken for her father's palliative influence to wear off.

Rachel tried to put the memories out of her head as she forced herself up the final few rungs and stepped into the attic. But the memories rose to slap her in the face.

A plastic drop cloth lay on the hard plank floor of the

attic, just as it had that night. And across the drop cloth, blood splashed in crimson streaks and puddles.

Fresh blood.

SETH HAD FOUND an old Dick Francis novel in one of the bookshelves and settled down to read, but his weariness and the rain's relentless cadence made it hard to stay awake. He'd closed his eyes for just a moment and suddenly he was back on the road to Smoky Joe's Saloon, the steel girders of Purgatory Bridge gleaming in his headlights.

He parked behind Rachel's Honda and got out, deeply aware of the brisk, cool wind whipping his hair and his clothes. It was strong. Too strong. It would fling Rachel right off the bridge if he didn't get to her.

But no matter how far he walked, she was still a few steps farther away, dancing gracefully along the narrow girder as if she were walking a tightwire. Her arms were out, her face raised to the sky, and she was humming a tune, something slow and vaguely familiar, like one of the classical pieces his sister had learned in her music class at school and tried to pick out on the old, out-of-tune upright piano that had belonged to his grandmother.

Suddenly, Rachel turned to look straight at him, her eyes wide and glittering in the faint light coming from the honky-tonk down the road.

"You can't save us all," she said.

A gust of wind slammed into his back, knocking him off balance and catching Rachel's clothes up in its swirling wake, flapping them like a sail. She lost her balance slowly, almost gracefully, and even though he threw himself forward, he couldn't stop her fall.

He crashed into the girder rail in time to hear her scream. It seemed to grow louder and louder, even as she fell farther and farther away. The thirty-foot gorge became a bottomless chasm, and the scream went on and on....

He woke with a start, just in time to hear a scream cut off, followed by dreadful silence.

Chapter Seven

Taking the stairs two at a time, Seth reached the second-floor landing in seconds. Down the hall, Rachel lay in a crumpled heap at the bottom of a ladder dropped down from an opening in the ceiling.

"Rachel!" Ignoring the aches and pains playing chase through his joints and muscles, he hurried to her side, nearly wilting with relief when she sat up immediately, staring at him with wide, scared eyes. "Are you okay? Are you hurt?"

"I don't know." She sounded winded. "I don't know if I'm okay."

She looked terrified, as if she'd been chased down the ladder by a monster. Tremors rolled through her slim body like a dozen small earthquakes going on inside her, making her teeth rattle. Her fingers dug into his arms.

He wrapped her in a bear hug, cocooning her against his body. She melted into him, clinging like a child.

What the hell had she seen?

"I need to go downstairs," she moaned. "Please, I can't be up here."

He helped her to her feet and led her down to the den, looking around desperately for a bar service. "Do you have any brandy?"

She shook her head as she sat on the sofa. "Dad had liver cancer. We all stopped drinking after the diagnosis."

Of course. "Okay, well, maybe some hot tea."

As he started to get up from where he crouched in front of her, she grabbed his hands and held him in place. "Don't go."

"Okay." He settled back into his crouch, stroking her cold fingers between his. "Can you at least tell me what happened?"

"I don't know."

But he could see she did know. She just didn't want to tell him.

A hank of hair had fallen into her face, hiding half her expression from him. He pushed it gently back behind her ear. "Maybe you had a bad dream?"

She shook her head.

"Not a dream?"

She looked less certain this time when she shook her head. "I don't think it was. I've never sleepwalked before."

"Then it probably wasn't a dream," he agreed. The concession didn't seem to give her much comfort. "Do you remember why you went up the ladder? Does it lead to the attic?"

She nodded. "I was dozing. And then I heard the music."

A snippet of memory flashed in his head. Rachel, gliding precariously along the girder rail, humming a song to herself.

"Was it this song?" he asked, humming a few notes.

Her head whipped up, her eyes locking with his. "How did you know?"

The anger in her tone caught him off guard, and he

had to put one hand on the sofa to keep from toppling over. "I dreamed it. Just a minute ago."

Her eyes narrowed. "It's Chopin," she said tightly. "A nocturne. I heard it coming from the attic."

"So you went up to the attic to see where the music was coming from?"

Her lips trembled, and the bracing anger he'd seen in her blue eyes melted into dread. "I went up because I already knew where it was coming from."

He didn't know what she meant. "What did you find?"

"Everything but the body." Her gaze wandered, settling on some point far away.

He stared at her with alarm. "What body?"

Her gaze snapped back to his. "My mother's."

Letting her words sink in, he tried to remember what he knew about her mother's death. It had happened when she was young. He'd been a teenager himself, on the cusp of learning an exciting if larcenous new life at the feet of Cleve Calhoun. The death of some rich woman on the east side of town hadn't registered.

She'd killed herself, he knew. No other details had ever come out, so he'd figured she'd taken pills or slit her wrists or something.

If she'd killed herself in the attic, maybe she'd hung herself. "When you say everything was there but the body—"

"I mean everything," she said flatly. Her voice had gained strength, and her trembling had eased. "There was a plastic drop sheet, just like that night. She hated messes, so she was determined not to make one, even when—" Rachel stopped short, her throat bobbing as she swallowed hard. "The music playing was Chopin's nocturne. And afterward—the blood—"

Oh my God, he thought. *She saw it.*

"Did you find her?" he asked gently, hoping that was the extent of what she'd experienced that night, as bad as it must have been.

She looked up at him with haunted eyes. "I saw it happen."

He stared back at her a moment, finally understanding her reaction to whatever she'd witnessed up in the attic. "Oh, Rachel."

She looked away from him. "I saw it again. I know I saw it."

But she wasn't sure, he realized. She was doubting herself. Why?

"Do you want me to go take a look?" he offered.

Her gaze whipped back around to his. "You think I've lost my mind."

He didn't think that, although given her experience in the attic years ago and the stresses of the past few days, he had to wonder if she'd misinterpreted whatever it was she'd seen. "I just think I should take a look. Maybe there's an intruder in the house."

The idea of a third party in the house seemed not to have occurred to her, which made Seth wonder if she suspected him of trying to trick her. The wary looks she was sending his way weren't exactly reassuring. "I'll go with you."

He frowned. "Are you sure?"

She nodded quickly, her eyes narrowing.

It was a test, he realized. He'd been with her ever since she'd fallen out of the attic, so if he were the culprit, everything would be as she'd left it.

It was a chance he'd take. If someone was trying to gaslight her, he might still be in the house. They might still be in danger.

He climbed the ladder first. She waited until he'd

stepped into the attic to start up after him, clutching the rungs with whitened knuckles. She moved slowly, with care, giving him a few seconds to view the room without any comment from her.

It was a small space, rectangular, with a steeply peaked ceiling of exposed rafters. The floor was hardwood planks, unpolished and mostly unfinished, though in the center of the room, large splotches and splashes of dark red wood stain marred the planks.

He looked doubtfully at the stain. In the dim light from the single bare overhead bulb, the splotches of red *did* look like blood. But what about the drop cloth? That was a pretty significant detail for her to have conjured up with her imagination.

Except she hadn't, had she? She'd told him the drop cloth had existed. In the past, on the night of her mother's suicide.

"No." Behind him, Rachel let out a low moan.

He turned to find her staring at the wood stain, her head shaking from side to side.

"I saw the drop cloth," she said. "I did. And there was blood. Wet blood."

Seth looked back at the stain. It was clearly dry. No one would ever mistake it for wet blood. So either Rachel had imagined everything—

Or someone had been here in the attic with her, hiding, and removed the evidence after she'd run away from the terrifying sight.

"You don't believe me," she accused, color rising in her cheeks. "You think I'm crazy."

"No, I don't," he said firmly, hiding his doubts. Until this moment, except when she was clearly under the influence of some sort of drug, Rachel had seemed completely sane and lucid. Plus, he'd worked for her company for over a year now and watched her tackle the tasks of learning her father's lifework with determination and tenacity.

She deserved the benefit of the doubt.

"Where was the drop cloth?" he asked.

She waved toward the stained area. "Right there. Over that stain. It was stretched out flat, covered with blood. Splotches and puddles. Still wet."

She walked slowly to the center of the floor, gazing down at the stain. Her troubled expression made his chest tighten. "I didn't imagine it. I know I didn't."

Okay, Hammond, think. If you were trying to con her into believing she'd lost her mind, how would you go about it?

"Who has access to the house?"

She relaxed a little at his pragmatic question. "I do, of course. My stepmother, but she's in North Carolina. Her sister lives in Wilmington, and Diane went to spend a couple of weeks with her. I think my stepbrother, Paul, probably has a key. And my father used to keep a key in his office at the trucking company in case one of us locked ourselves out and there wasn't anyone else around."

"Do you know if it's still there?"

"I don't know. I was planning to go through my dad's office next week and see if there was anything else that needed to be handled." Grief darkened her eyes.

Impulsively, he pulled her into his arms.

She came willingly, pressing her face against the side of his throat. When she drew away from him, she seemed steadier on her feet. "You think someone set me up?"

"I've been asking myself what steps I'd take to try to convince you that you were losing your mind."

"You think that's what's going on?"

"Look at you just a few minutes ago. Shaking like a leaf and not sure you could trust your own eyes."

She looked stricken. Her reaction piqued his curiosity, but he kept his questions to himself. If it was something he needed to know, she'd tell him soon enough.

"Remember how I told you I thought those murders were part of trying to target you?"

She nodded, her expression guarded.

"What if the goal was to make you appear crazy?"

She didn't answer, but her eyes flickered with comprehension. It made sense to her, he realized. Maybe even seemed inevitable.

"Your mother was already dead, and your father was dying. If I were ruthless and wanted to make you doubt your sanity, I'd take steps to isolate you even further. I'd take away your support system. Amelia Sanderson had been your friend since you were both in college, right?" He had learned that much while nosing around town about the murders.

She nodded, a bleak look in her wintry eyes.

"April Billings was your first hire, and you saw a lot of yourself in her, didn't you?" He could tell by the shift in her expression that he'd gotten it right. He usually did, he thought with a hint of shame. It had been one of his most useful talents, his ability to read people, relationships and situations. "And you'd made Coral Vines your own personal rehabilitation project. You'd helped her find a grief counselor to deal with her pain about her husband's death. I bet you'd even given her information about a twelve-step program for her alcohol addiction."

"How do you know this?" she asked in a strangled voice.

"I used to do this for a living. Reading people. Finding out their secrets and figuring out their relationships so I could use the knowledge to my advantage."

She couldn't stop her lip from curling with distaste, though she schooled her expression quickly. It didn't matter. He felt enough disgust for his past for the both of them. "And Marjorie was like a mom to me," she added, filling in the next obvious blank. "My mentor."

"But you still didn't break, did you?" He touched her face before he realized he was going to. He dropped his hand quickly, bracing himself for her rebuke.

But all she did was smile a shaky smile. "No, I didn't break."

"I don't think it's a coincidence you were drugged the night of your father's funeral. You were as vulnerable as you'd ever been at that moment, I would guess. He couldn't let the opportunity pass."

"This doesn't make any sense. It never has. Your sister said she thought these murders were about me, and you said it, too, but why? Why would you think it? Just because I knew them?" She shook her head, clearly not wanting to believe it. "I saw the stories in the papers—Mark Bramlett was connected to serial murders in Nashville, too. What makes you think he was anything more than a sick freak who got off on killing women? Why does everyone think someone hired him?"

She didn't know about Mark Bramlett's last words, he realized. The police hadn't told her.

"I was there when Mark Bramlett died," he said.

"What? Why?"

"I'd tracked down the truck Bramlett used for the murders to help Sutton Calhoun find Ivy Hawkins. You remember Sutton, right? The guy who was investigating April Billings's murder?"

She nodded. "Yeah, he and Ivy came to me for a list of

the trucks we rented out. That's how they found Bramlett."

"I wanted to know why Bramlett killed those women. I knew them all, you know. Amelia was always kind to me, and she didn't have to be. April Billings was full of life and so much potential. I grew up with Coral Vines on Smoky Ridge. She was the sweetest kid there ever was, and after her husband died, I tried to help her out with things around her house she couldn't do herself."

"I didn't know."

"Marjorie Kenner tried to steer me right, back in school. I didn't listen, but I never forgot that she tried." He thought about the kindhearted high school librarian who'd fought for his soul and lost. "I wanted justice for them, too. I wanted to see Bramlett pay."

"Did you?"

He nodded slowly. "I watched him die. But before he went, he said something."

She closed her hand around his wrist, her fingers digging urgently into his flesh. "What?"

"I'd told Ivy Hawkins I thought you were his real target. And as he died, he told her I was right. He said, 'It's all about the girl.'"

Rachel looked horrified. "He said that? Why did no one tell me?"

"I don't know. But I can probably get in touch with Ivy Hawkins if you want confirmation."

Rachel turned away from him, her gaze moving over the attic, settling finally on a darkened corner. "I wonder—" She walked toward the corner, leaving Seth to catch up. "Do you have a light?"

He pulled his keys from his pocket and engaged the small flashlight he kept on the keychain. The narrow beam of light drove shadows out of the dark corner, revealing another trapdoor in the attic floor.

And wedged in the narrow seam of the door was a thin piece of torn plastic.

As Rachel reached out for it, Seth caught her hand. "Fingerprints."

She looked up at him, a gleam of relief in her eyes. "It's from the drop cloth. It was really here." She tried to tug the door open, but it didn't budge.

Seth reached into another pocket and pulled out his Swiss Army knife. Tucked into one compartment in the case was a small pair of tweezers. He used them to pluck the piece of plastic out of the trapdoor seam.

The flimsy plastic was shaped like a triangle, smooth on two sides and ragged on the third, where it had apparently ripped away from the bigger sheet of plastic. In one corner of the plastic, a drop of red liquid was almost dry. Seth caught a quick whiff of a sharp iron odor.

"Is that—"

He nodded. "Blood."

She put her hand over her mouth.

"Rachel, whoever did this could still be in the house."

Her eyes went wide. "Oh my God."

"Where does this trapdoor lead?"

"A mudroom off the kitchen, I think. I've never used this exit, but there's a trapdoor in the ceiling of that room."

"Are there any weapons in this house?"

She swallowed hard. "My dad had a Glock. He kept it in his bedroom drawer. I guess it's still there."

"Do you know how to use it?"

She looked sick. "Yes."

"Let's get you downstairs and locked in that room. Then I'll take a look around."

"Don't you need the gun, then?"

He shook his head. "With my record, a gun is more trouble than it's worth." He had the Swiss Army knife, and he was pretty good at fighting with whatever weapons he could find. Unless their intruder was carrying a gun himself—and Seth had a feeling he wasn't—Seth would be safe enough. He wasn't the target. Rachel was.

Rachel appeared unnerved until they reached the second-floor hallway, clear of the ladder. She seemed to calm down once she was on solid ground.

She unlocked her father's gun from its case and, with more or less steady hands, went about the task of loading ammunition into the magazine while Seth watched. She met his gaze with scared but determined eyes. "Done."

"I'll be right back." He closed the door behind him, waiting until he heard her engage the lock before he went in search of the intruder.

The stairs creaked as he descended to the first floor, making him wince. He paused at the bottom and listened carefully for any sound of movement. He heard rain battering the windows and siding. Electricity humming in the walls. His own quickened breathing.

But no other sounds.

He crossed the main hallway, checking room by room until he was satisfied they were empty. Reaching the kitchen, he stood in the center of the warm room, struck unexpectedly by the memory of his body brushing against Rachel's here earlier that afternoon, back when his worst worry was whether or not his body betrayed his unanticipated arousal.

He'd give anything to go back to that moment right about now.

The mudroom was off the kitchen, she'd said. He went to the small door on the other side of the refrigerator and listened through the wood for any sound on the other side. He heard nothing but silence.

Backtracking to the kitchen counter, he went to the knife block by the sink and selected a long fillet knife. He crossed back to the mudroom, gripped the knife tightly in his right hand and opened the door.

Nobody jumped him as he entered. The room was empty.

He looked for signs of recent occupation. At first glance, the room appeared undisturbed. No mud on the floor, no telltale drops of blood from the drop cloth the intruder must have taken with him.

But there wouldn't be, would there? That had been the point of the drop cloth, to keep the evidence contained for easy, complete removal. Rachel's tormenter wanted her to doubt her own mind, which meant he couldn't leave any clues behind.

Maybe he'd heard Seth's voice earlier, outside the attic when he'd first responded to Rachel's cries. That might have pushed him to make a hasty exit at the first opportunity, which had come when Seth had taken Rachel to the den to recover from the shock of what she'd seen.

The intruder had moved fast, rolling up the drop cloth and the evidence it contained, and made a quick escape through the mudroom hatch. But in his haste, he hadn't realized one corner of the drop cloth had snagged in the trapdoor seam.

Had he taken the time to fold the drop cloth into a more manageable square before he left the attic? Possibly not. Which meant he'd have been moving at a clip, trying to get out of the house before he was discovered. Maybe he'd left other evidence behind besides the torn piece of plastic sheeting.

The back door was locked when Seth tried the handle,

but anyone with a key could have locked it behind him as he left. Using the hem of his borrowed T-shirt, Seth turned the dead bolt and opened the door to the backyard. Beyond the mudroom door, he found a flagstone patio, not the muddy ground as he'd hoped. Not that it would have mattered, he supposed. With the rain coming down in torrents, any footprints the intruder might have left would have been obliterated in seconds.

He closed the door against the driving rain and turned, looking at the mudroom from a different angle. The room was essentially bare of furnishings save for a low, built-in bench with storage space beneath. There was nothing in any of the storage bins, suggesting the room was rarely used.

He looked at the trapdoor in the mudroom ceiling. It was two floors down from the attic. What lay between the attic trap door and the one in the mudroom?

Only one way to find out.

He caught the latch and pulled the trapdoor open. A wooden ladder unfolded and dropped to the ground.

Tightening his grip on the knife, he stepped onto the ladder and started to climb.

Chapter Eight

Seth had been gone forever, hadn't he? Rachel checked her watch and saw that only a few minutes had passed.

Time crawls when you're scared witless.

She had settled on the cedar chest at the foot of her father's bed, trying not to think about his final moments here, as he breathed his last, labored breaths and finally let go.

Someone had changed the sheets and neatened the room after the coroner's visit. She and Diane had both been far too shattered to have thought of such a thing, so it must have been Paul. He'd been a rock for them both, a steady hand here at home and at the trucking company, as well.

He hadn't always been a big fan of his mother's second marriage—he'd worried that their relationship would make things awkward between him and her father at work, for one thing—but for the past few months, as her father fought the cancer that had ultimately taken him, Paul had put in a lot of long hours at work, helping take up the slack.

She wasn't sure what she'd have done without him. So why hadn't she called him to help her this morning instead of depending on strangers? Why did she feel certain, even now, that a man as enigmatic and unpredictable as Seth Hammond was the best person to help her?

A noise coming from the other side of the room froze her midthought. She picked up the gun from where she'd set it on the cedar chest beside her and turned toward the sound.

There. It came again. It sounded like footsteps coming from just inside her father's closet.

Then came the rattle of the doorknob turning.

Her chest tightening, Rachel lifted the small pistol, trying to remember what she knew about a good shooting stance. She hadn't done enough shooting to internalize these rules, damn it! Why hadn't she practiced more? What was the point of learning to shoot if you couldn't remember the lessons when it counted?

Fighter's stance, her sluggish brain shouted. Weak foot forward, strong foot back and slightly out, lean into the shot.

The door opened slowly, and Rachel's heart skipped a beat.

Seth Hammond emerged from the darkened closet, spotted the barrel of the gun aimed squarely at his chest and immediately ducked and rolled.

He hissed a profanity from behind the bed. "I think I just lost ten years of my life!"

She laid the gun on the chest and hurried around to where he crouched, his head down and his chest heaving. "How did you get into that closet?"

"That's where the trapdoor in the mudroom leads," he told her, lifting his head to look at her. "There's a hatch in the top of the closet that leads up to the attic. It has a pin lock hasp—that's why you couldn't open it from the attic."

Of course, she thought. There was a whole level between the attic and the mudroom. Why hadn't she thought of that?

He pushed to his feet. "I didn't find any evidence downstairs in the mudroom, but I couldn't find a light in the closet for a look around."

"There's a light switch, but it's in a weird place." She opened the closet door and reached inside, feeling for the switch positioned inside one of the built-in shoe hutches. The overhead light came on, revealing the roomy walk-in closet her father and Diane had shared during their marriage.

Diane's belongings took up most of the room, with her father's clothes and shoes filling only a quarter of the space. The area was neat and organized, Rachel knew, because while Diane could be flighty about many things, she was dead serious about her clothes and accessories, and she kept her things where she could locate them with a quick glance.

Which made the shoe box jutting at an odd angle from one of the shelves seem all the more out of place.

Rachel crossed to the box and saw that the top was slightly displaced, as well. And on the corner of the bright yellow box, a dark crimson smear was still glistening, not quite dry.

"More blood," she murmured, feeling ill.

Seth came up behind her, a solid wall of reassuring heat. She squelched the urge to lean back against him, aware that she was already leaning on him more than was probably wise.

He seemed remarkably steady for a man who'd sustained a head injury just a few hours earlier, showing few signs of pain or disorientation since he'd come here with her. On the contrary, he'd been a rock just as she'd had her feet knocked out from beneath her.

What if that's not a coincidence?

She shook off the thought. Seth had earned a little trust from her, hadn't he? A little benefit of the doubt.

"There was a lot of blood on that drop cloth," she said aloud. "Too much."

"May not be human, though." Seth's voice was reassuring. "It wouldn't have to be. Easy enough to get animal blood to set this up, and you could do it without breaking any laws."

She turned to look at him. "He's worried about breaking the law?"

"Never break the law if you don't have to. First rule of the con game."

"I thought the first rule of the con game was that you couldn't con an honest man." She wasn't sure where she'd heard that, but she'd always considered it to be a reasonable assumption. Honest men didn't fall for deals that were too good to be true.

Seth shook his head. "Honest men can be conned. Everyone has a price, even if the price is honorable." He grimaced. "I guess never breaking the law if you don't have to isn't necessarily the first rule of the con game, but it was the first rule Cleve Calhoun taught me."

She didn't miss the hint of affection in his voice when he spoke of his old mentor. He may have walked away from the life Calhoun had taught him, but clearly he hadn't stopped caring about the old man.

"Whoever's behind this isn't used to skirting the law," he added.

"How can you say that? He's already hired someone to kill four women. He's drugged me and probably killed Davis Rogers—oh God." Her voice cracked. "Davis. I wonder if the police have found him yet."

"I think we'd have already heard from them if they had."

She closed her eyes, fighting off her growing despair. She needed to stay strong. Not let this mess destroy her.

Not again.

"What I meant about this guy not being used to breaking the law is he's hired other people to do it so far," Seth added quietly.

"What makes you think he didn't beat up Davis himself?"

"If he was a practiced killer, he'd have killed those women himself. But he didn't. He hired someone else to do it. He doesn't want his hands dirty if he can avoid it."

Rachel heard something in Seth's voice that pinged her radar, but he spoke again before she could pin it down.

"What do you want to do now?" he asked.

"I think we need to call the police."

He nodded, though he clearly found the idea unappealing. "Okay. But call Antoine Parsons directly, not nine-one-one."

That made sense—Antoine already knew the details of the case. He seemed fair and honest, too. "You don't have to be here for it," she offered, aware that he still looked uncomfortable.

He shot her a sheepish grin. "Yeah, I do. I'm a material witness."

She started toward the phone but stopped halfway, turning back to look at him. "Seth, do you have any idea who's doing this?"

"Who's doing it? No." He shook his head firmly. "But I have an idea *why* he's doing it."

To Antoine Parson's credit, he didn't automatically start grilling Seth about why he'd been there with Rachel when the craziness started. First, he caught them up on the search for Davis Rogers. "We've searched the woods behind the bed-and-breakfast, but there's a lot of wilderness to cover in that area, and if the point of knocking out Mr. Hammond was to keep him from calling the paramedics to help Rogers, it's unlikely they'd hide the body anywhere near those woods."

Rachel flinched at his use of the word *body*. Seth's chest ached in sympathy, and he barely kept himself from giving her a comforting hug.

"We've also contacted the police in Virginia to let them know we have a report that Rogers is missing," Antoine added. "If he contacts his family or any of his friends back home, they've been asked to let us know."

Antoine had brought along a uniformed police officer to help him with the interviews. The two of them separated Seth and Rachel to get their independent statements.

Antoine took Seth's, naturally. But to Seth's relief, he approached his questions in a straightforward way and seemed to believe Seth's answers. "Bold, just walking in here and setting something up that way," the detective remarked. "Especially with you both right here in the house."

"I'm not sure whoever did this knew I was here," Seth said. "My car's in the shop having the tires fixed. The only car here is Rachel's. He might have assumed she was alone."

Antoine gave a slow nod. "And you didn't see anything of what Ms. Davenport saw in the attic?"

"Just the piece of drop cloth plastic I gave you and a stain on a shoe box in the closet that might be blood. But I think I did hear the music that Rachel heard playing." He told Antoine about his dream, leaving out the part about Rachel on the bridge girder. "I know it was just a dream, but how did I dream that particular song at that particular time?"

"Would be a hell of a coincidence," Antoine agreed. "Do you think this is connected to the previous murders?"

"Of course."

"Of course." Antoine looked thoughtful. "What's in this for you, Hammond?"

Ah, Seth thought. *Now we get to the grilling part.* "I knew the murder victims. I liked them, and I like Rachel Davenport, too. Her father took a chance on me when he hired me at the trucking company when most people around here wouldn't spit on me if I was on fire."

Antoine smiled a little. "I wish I could feel sorry for you, but…"

"I'm not the bad guy here."

"No, I don't think you are," Antoine agreed.

The other policeman, Gavin McElroy, joined Antoine in a huddle near the doorway of the den, leaving Seth and Rachel alone across the room.

Seth crossed to where she stood near the windows, rubbing her arms as if she was cold. "You okay?"

"Yeah." She managed a smile. "I'm sure I sounded crazy to poor Officer McElroy."

He heard a faint undertone to her words that was beginning to make a bleak sort of sense to him. She was very concerned about appearing sane, understandably. After all, her mother had committed suicide.

"You're not crazy," he told her firmly. The look of gratitude she sent his way made his stomach hurt.

Did she fear her mother's instability was hereditary? She wasn't much younger than her mother had been when she'd died. It was probably something she worried about now and then.

Maybe more often than now and then.

Did the person now tormenting her know that she harbored such a fear? The two direct attacks on her so far seemed aimed less at hurting her than convincing her she was losing her mind—first the drugging incident, inducing a state of near psychosis, then the gaslighting attempt in the attic, designed to make her believe she was seeing things that didn't exist.

Going back even further, the murders of people who'd been important to her seemed ominously significant now, too. If he'd wanted to drive Rachel to mental instability, he could think of no better way to prepare the ground than to brutally eliminate all of her emotional underpinnings. Every one of those murders had been a powerful blow to Rachel Davenport. Could that effect have been their entire purpose?

"You said you thought you knew why someone is targeting me," Rachel murmured, keeping her voice too low for Antoine and Gavin to hear. "Did you tell Detective Parsons?"

"Not yet. I wanted to run it by you first."

"You could have told me before they got here." She sounded a little annoyed. He'd kept his thoughts to himself while they'd waited because he needed to think through his suspicions before he committed to them. If he was wrong, he might be pushing the investigation in the wrong direction, putting Rachel in graver danger.

But after talking to Antoine, and realizing the police didn't have a clue what was driving the attacks surrounding Rachel, he was growing more certain he was right.

Someone wanted Rachel out of the way, and he was pretty sure it had everything to do with Davenport Trucking.

"If you were to resign as CEO of Davenport Trucking tomorrow, who becomes CEO?" he asked quietly.

She shot him a puzzled look. "There's a trustee board my father set up before he died. If something happened to me, they would make the decision, I think. I don't know. My father knew I was committed to running his company. I gave him my word."

"But accidents happen. People get high and fall off bridges, right?"

Her gaze snapped up again. "You think all of this is about getting me out of the way at Davenport?"

"What if you were deemed mentally unstable? Would that get you out of the way?"

She looked horrified. "Probably."

Antoine and Officer McElroy walked back to where they stood, ending the conversation for the moment. "We'll get a lab crew here later as soon as we can to process the access points to the attic," Antoine told them. "Meanwhile, Officer McElroy is going to stay here to preserve the chain of evidence until they arrive."

"Do we have to stay here?" Rachel asked bluntly.

Antoine looked surprised. "No, I don't suppose so, but I'm not sure you should be out on the roads in this weather."

"I don't plan to go far." She gave Seth an imperious look that did more to relieve his worries about her mental state than anything he'd seen so far. She looked like a pissed-off warrior princess, one he had a feeling he'd follow to the end of the universe if that's what she desired.

He was in serious, serious trouble.

THE CABIN NEAR the base of Copperhead Ridge had been in her father's family since her great-grandfather had built it with his own hands in the late twenties. Or so the story went. Rachel looked at the slightly shabby facade with a fond smile as she pulled the Honda into the gravel driveway near the front door.

"What is this place?" Seth had been quiet for most of the short drive, but once she killed the engine, his low drawl broke the silence.

"According to family lore, my great-grandfather built this place to cover a family moonshining operation during Prohibition." She slanted a look his way. "I'm not sure that's entirely true."

He met her look with a hint of a smile. "Good stories rarely are."

"I think it might have been embellished to give the Davenports a little hillbilly cred." She smiled. "We were damned Yankees, you see. My great-grandfather was the third son of a shipbuilding family in Maryland that had only enough money to support two sons. So he was left to find his own way in the cold, cruel world."

"And chose Bitterwood, Tennessee?" Seth gave her a skeptical look.

"There's beauty here, you know. It's not all harsh."

"Guess it depends on what part of Bitterwood you come from."

She conceded the point. "My grandfather told me his daddy knew from the moment he set eyes on Bitterwood that it was home."

Seth's expression softened. "I guess I can't argue with that. I always end up back here no matter how far I roam."

"I love this place." She nodded toward the cabin. "My grandmother was a Bitterwood native. Her roots go back to the first settlers. She and my grandfather would bring me here during summer vacations from school and we'd rough it." She laughed. "Well, I considered it roughing it."

In fact, for a primitive log cabin, the place was relatively luxurious. A removable window unit air conditioner cooled the place in the heat of summer, and a woodstove kept it cozy on all but the coldest of winter days. It had been wired with electricity a couple of decades ago, when the town borders extended close enough to the cabin to make it feasible. And with a nearby cell tower, she never had much trouble getting a phone signal.

Seth climbed the porch steps behind her, carrying their bags. She'd packed a few things before leaving her house, and they'd stopped by the bungalow on Smoky Ridge where Seth lived in order to pick up clothes for him, as well.

The shabby old house belonged to Cleve Calhoun, the con man who'd brought Seth into that lifestyle, Seth had told her, his expression defensive. He'd moved in with Cleve again a few years back, after the older man had suffered a debilitating stroke. Now that Cleve was at a rehab center in Knoxville for the next few weeks, Seth was thinking about looking for a place of his own.

Rachel wondered what sort of place a man like Seth would like, watching with curiosity as his sharp green eyes took in the decor of the cabin. She'd decorated it herself several years ago, when her grandfather had left it to her in his will. She'd been twenty-two, fresh out of college and torn between sadness at one part of her life passing and a whole vista of opportunity spreading out before her.

As a permanent place of residence, the cabin posed too many problems to be practical, but she had always treated it as an escape when life started to become overwhelming.

Was that why she'd come here now?

"Nice digs," he said with a faint smile.

"I love this place," she admitted.

"I can see why." He looked at her. "Do you come here often?"

"When I need to."

He nodded as if he understood. "Why did you bring me here? You don't bring people here normally, do you?"

She looked at him through narrowed eyes, a little spooked by how easily he could read her. "No, I don't."

"Because it's a refuge."

"Yes." She felt naked.

Suddenly, he looked vulnerable, as well. "Thank you. For trusting me enough to bring me here."

His rapid change of demeanor caught her by surprise. She hadn't realized, until that moment, that she had any sort of power over him. He'd seemed so sure, so in charge, that she hadn't given any thought to being able to influence him in any way.

It was an unexpectedly heady feeling, one that made her feel reckless.

And alive.

He was beautiful, she thought, standing there in the middle of her haven. Beautiful and feral, constantly on the edge of flight. Despite the facade of civilization, despite his obvious attempts to fight his own wild instincts, he would never be fully tame. He would never be genteel or domesticated. He'd always be a wild card.

And she'd never wanted a man more than she wanted him, in spite of that unpredictability.

Or maybe because of it.

"I wanted you here with me," she said aloud, unsure that he would understand what she meant by it. Not sure she wanted him to.

But she should have known better. He had a wild thing's instinct for reading another creature's motives.

Fight or flight, she thought. Which would he choose? To run?

Or to engage?

When he moved, it was swift and fierce, the decisive action of a predator with a singular purpose. He came to an abrupt stop in front of her, his gaze so intense it set off tremors low in her belly. "Do you know what you're getting into?"

Probably not, but she had no intention of retreating. "Do you?"

His mouth curved in response. She imagined the feel of those lips on hers, and the tremors inside her spread in waves until she felt as if she were going to crumble apart.

Then he touched her, a light brush of fingertips against her jaw, sparking fire in her blood.

She rose, closing the space between them until her breasts flattened against his chest. His wiry arms ensnared her, crushing her even closer, until his breath heated her cheeks. "I'm dangerous," he whispered.

She met his gaze. "I know."

Threading her fingers through his crisp, dark hair, she kissed him.

Chapter Nine

Her mouth was hot and sweet, the fierce thrust of her tongue against his pouring gasoline on the fire in his belly until he thought he'd explode. He wanted her more than anything he'd ever wanted his whole life, a realization that scared the hell out of him even as it drove him to walk her backward until they ran up against the cabin wall.

She made a low, explosive sound against his mouth as her back flattened against the polished logs. Her legs parted, making room for his hips to settle flush to hers, and any hope of hiding the effect she had on his body was gone as he thrust helplessly against her hips. Neither the borrowed sweatpants nor her thin cotton yoga pants offered much of a barrier between their bodies, making it all too easy to take what they both seemed desperately to want.

Stop, his mind begged him. *Think.*

There was a reason he was still alone, a reason why he hadn't coaxed one of the pretty Tennessee mountain girls to take a chance on a man like him. Even reformed, he wasn't much of a catch. He was rough around the edges and wild at heart. A girl willing to settle for less than perfect could still do better.

Rachel Davenport didn't have to settle. If all she

wanted was a quick roll in the hay with a hard-bodied redneck, maybe he'd give it a go, but not when she was this vulnerable. Not the day after her father's funeral, the day she'd lost another man who was important to her.

Not the day she'd had a nerve-shattering scare and probably wanted nothing more than to feel something besides fear.

As he started to pull back, her hands moved with sureness over his body, sliding down his back to cup his buttocks, pulling him closer. For a second, everything resembling lucid thought rushed out of his head, driven away by raw male hunger for completion. He drove his hips against hers again, making her whimper. The sound was maddening, fueling his lust to the edge of control.

She tugged his shirt upward, baring his belly to the light caress of her fingertips. She dragged her mouth away from his and pressed a hot kiss against the center of his chest, her tongue dancing lightly over the curve of his pectoral muscle.

She looked up at him, her blue eyes drunk with desire. "Is that good?" she asked, her thumb tracing a circle around his left nipple. "Did you like that?"

"Yes," he breathed.

She bent her head and dropped a soft kiss along the ridge of his rib cage. "And that?"

He knew where she was headed. He knew if he let her keep going, he wouldn't be able to make any sort of coherent decision about right and wrong.

There had been a time, he realized, when the question of right and wrong wouldn't have occurred to him at all.

Did he really want to be that man again?

With a groan, he threaded his fingers through her hair and urged her to look up at him. She appeared confused but also wildly aroused, her cheeks flushed and dewy, her lips dark from his kisses.

He kissed her again, a long, slow kiss that had an oddly fortifying effect on his resolve. Rachel Davenport deserved to be wooed, with kisses that went somewhere besides straight to sex.

Even if he wasn't the man who could give her that.

When he let her go, she slumped back against the wall, staring at him through half-closed eyes. Her breath was swift and ragged, her hair a tangled curtain around her face. "Seth?"

"This isn't really what you want," he said, keeping a careful distance.

Her brow furrowed. "You don't get to make that decision."

"Okay. It isn't what *I* want."

Her gaze dropped pointedly to his sweatpants, where his body betrayed exactly what he wanted. When her blue eyes rose to meet his again, there was triumph in them. "Really."

"Rachel, please." He turned his back on her, pacing toward the front window, where night had fallen early due to the rain. His reflection stared back at him, the wild-eyed gaze of a man on the edge.

"If you think you're being noble—"

"I don't think I'm capable of being noble. I just want to be fair."

She let out an exasperated sigh. "You think I'm not in my right mind."

He shook his head, even though it was what he thought, in a way. "I think we both want to forget the past couple of days, however we can make that happen. And maybe that seems like a good idea right now, but it won't once we've crossed a line we can't uncross."

He waited for her to respond, but she remained silent. Finally, he dared a quick look at her. She still leaned against the wall, her gaze on him. Some of the heat in her eyes had died, however, as if his words had sunk in and extinguished the fire inside her.

"I don't do one-night stands," she admitted after another long, silent moment. "I don't think that's how I was looking at this."

He didn't know if her confession made him feel better or worse. Maybe a little of both, he decided, though her admission that she saw him as more than a body on which to slake her lust certainly complicated matters.

"I'm not good for you," he said simply.

"You're not bad for me."

He laughed a little. "There are hundreds of people out there who'd beg to differ."

"You've done bad things. But you're not bad. Bad people don't try to change. They don't see the need."

He felt enough in control to face her completely. He pressed his back against the hardwood frame around the panes, concentrating on the discomfort and giving his body a chance to cool down and regain control. "There'↘ difference between wanting to be good and being go↘

"Only in degrees."

She was stubborn, he thought. And naive. "I↘ days, once we figure all this out, you're going ↘ back at this moment and thank me for keeping ↘

Her eyes rolled upward. "You give me a↘ that paternalistic hogwash and it won't take↘

Fair enough, he thought. "I don't want r↘

The look she shot his way was utterly ↘ ing him by surprise. "You wouldn't ha↘

He laughed. "Maybe not."

She lifted her chin, her expressi↘

cool neutral. "Okay. I get that this is a volatile situation with really rotten timing. And I know we're not what anyone would consider a suitable match. So, you win. We don't let this happen again, not while we're trying to figure out what's happening to me and why."

He felt a squirm of disappointment that she'd conceded so quickly, but he pushed that unhelpful thought aside. "I do think someone should be with you at all times, though. You've already had two strange incidents on top of whatever happened to your friend Davis, plus the previous murders. I don't think it's safe for you to be alone right now."

"Should I hire a bodyguard?" She sounded reluctant.

Seth thought about his orders from Adam Brand. Brand, for reasons Seth didn't quite understand, had hired Seth to keep an eye on Rachel. So far, he hadn't shared that fact with her, since Brand hadn't given him permission to approach her on an official level.

But maybe it was time to talk to Brand again. He was overdue to give the man an update. He'd try to make the FBI agent see that Rachel deserved to know everything that was going on.

"I can do it," he said in answer to her question. "I can protect you."

Her dark eyebrows notched up. "I thought we decided o keep our distance from each other."

"We agreed not to…get busy with each other," he said ith a wry grin. "Not quite the same thing."

"One would certainly make the other harder to resist."

True, but letting Rachel Davenport out of his sight for was not something he was willing to contemplate. ight not understand Brand's interest in Rachel, but derstood his own. He wasn't going to let her become alty in whatever game her tormenter was playing.

Especially now that he had a pretty good idea why she'd been targeted.

But before he told her his theory, he needed to talk to Brand. The FBI agent could pull some strings and see if the local cops were making any progress in finding Davis Rogers, for one thing. Antoine had claimed to be forthcoming, but Seth didn't kid himself. The cops would never trust him, not really, and nothing guaranteed Antoine would keep him in the loop.

Seth had a feeling what happened to Rogers might be more than just collateral damage aimed at weakening Rachel's hold on reality. Rogers had seen her the night before, at Smoky Joe's. What if he'd seen or heard something that could incriminate the person who was really behind these attacks on her?

"Rachel, this morning at Sequoyah House, you said you talked to Davis Rogers before you heard the thud and his phone cut off, right?"

She looked puzzled by the change of topic. "I didn't really understand what he meant by what he was saying, but I guess he must have met me last night at some point. He said something about being sorry about what he did."

Joe Breslin had said the man Rachel was with had made a pass at her. Could that have been why Davis Rogers had felt the need to apologize? "Can you remember what he said exactly?"

Her brow furrowed. "He said he'd been trying to reach me—I guess that makes sense. My phone was locked in my car. Then he said he needed to apologize about last night—oh!" She crossed to where she'd laid her fleece jacket on the back of the sofa and pulled her cell phone from the pocket. "I played this for the police but not for you."

She punched a couple of buttons and a male voice

came out of the phone's tinny speaker. "Rachel, it's Davis again. Look, I'm sorry about last night, but he seemed to think you might be receptive. I've really missed you. I didn't like leaving you in that place. Please call me back so I can apologize."

"*He* thought you might be receptive," Seth repeated. That jibed with what Joe had told him, but who was the "he" Rogers had been talking about?

"I think maybe he tried to kiss me or something."

"And you didn't let him."

She shot Seth a look. "I broke up with Davis years ago. I still care about him, and I desperately hope you're wrong about how bad his condition was and that we find him alive and okay. But I'm not in love with him anymore."

"Is he in love with you?"

"I don't think he ever was," she said flatly. "I'm not sure Davis loves anyone quite as much as he loves himself." She pressed her fingers against her lips. "God, that sounds terrible, especially since he could be dead because he came here to see me."

"Remember how I told you I went to talk to Smoky Joe this morning, and that's how I knew to look for Davis?"

She nodded.

"Joe said the man you were with made a pass at you, and you rebuffed him. I figure that man must have been Davis Rogers."

"Why didn't you tell me before?"

"I thought it was something you'd prefer to remember on your own."

Her expression took on a slightly haughty air, reminding him that no matter how tempting he might find her, and how receptive she might be, there was a whole lifetime of differences between them, in experiences, in education, in culture and in outlook. "You had no right to make that decision for me."

"Won't happen again," he snapped back.

She closed her eyes. "I'm sorry. I shouldn't have barked at you."

His anger ebbed as quickly as it had risen. He had no right to get up on his high horse considering he was still keeping the secret about Adam Brand. "No harm done."

"I wonder what he meant—that 'he' seemed to think I might be receptive to Davis's advances," Rachel murmured thoughtfully. "Who's the 'he' Davis is talking about?"

"I was wondering that, too."

"I don't think Davis knows anyone here in Bitterwood besides me. I mean, he knew my dad, of course, but my father's dead. I guess he might have met Diane once—she and my dad married around the time Davis and I broke up—"

"What about your stepbrother?"

"Paul?" She frowned. "I don't think so. We've gotten fairly friendly over the past few months, dealing with the company and taking care of my father's last wishes, but—" She shook her head. "We were both adults when our parents met. We didn't form any kind of family bond, and I can't imagine him giving Davis advice about my love life."

Bailey didn't seem the matchmaker type, Seth conceded. Or the criminal type. He was an efficient, if perpetually distracted, office manager, helping George Davenport and his daughter keep the company going. But company scuttlebutt notwithstanding, Seth had never thought Paul seemed to want to run the company.

But someone did.

"How can we find out who's next in line for the CEO job if you can't step in?" he asked.

Rachel looked up at him. "The only thing I know for sure is that, until my father's will is executed and I'm declared in charge, the company is under the control of a trust. And even then, the trust managers can make a change within the first year if I were to die. In other words, I can't put the disposition of the CEO job in my own will until I've run the company for at least a year."

"What if you couldn't take the job from the outset?"

"I don't know. It hasn't been an issue, since I already agreed to take on the responsibility."

"Do you regret it?" he asked out of curiosity.

"Agreeing to run the company?" Her brow furrowed, and she gave the question the thought it deserved. "I don't regret keeping my father's company alive. I don't regret the time I spent with my dad learning the ropes, or the peace it gave him to know the company would be staying in the family."

"That's not entirely what I asked."

"I miss being a librarian," she admitted with a faint smile. "But I can volunteer on weekends. Or take time out to go read to the kids on story day."

"Is that enough?"

"It will be." Her voice was firm. "It has to be."

A shrill noise split the tense silence that fell briefly between them. They both reached for their cell phones.

It was Rachel's phone. "Hello?"

She listened for a moment, her expression so tight it made Seth's chest hurt. "Yes, I understand." Another brief pause and she added, "Yes. I can do that. Okay. Thank you."

She hung up the phone, her expression carefully still as she slowly lifted her gaze to meet Seth's. What her features lacked in expressiveness, her blue eyes made up for, blazing with pain and fear.

"What is it?" he asked carefully.

Her throat bobbed with a deep swallow. "That was Antoine Parsons. A motorist on the Great Smoky Mountains Parkway pulled over near Sevierville to take a picture of the mountains and spotted a man's body lying about twenty feet down an incline. The Sevier County police called the Bitterwood P.D. because of the APB they'd put out on Davis."

"Is it him?"

"He didn't have any identification on him, but he does have a few identifying marks. They want me to take a look at the body and see if it's him."

"No," he said flatly.

Her eyebrows lifted. "No?"

"They can't ask you to look at a body like that," he said firmly, remembering how the man in the bushes had looked. His recall of the event had been coming back to him slowly but surely, and what he remembered of the man's condition only strengthened his resolve. "The man I saw in the bushes was badly beaten. You might not even be able to recognize him—his face was a mess—"

"I don't think it's his face they want me to look at," she said quietly. "He has birthmarks and scars on his body that I'd be able to identify."

The sudden, entirely inappropriate flood of jealousy burning through his system only made him angrier—at himself, at the police for putting her in such a horrible position and, most of all, at the monster who was wreaking havoc all around her life for what seemed, to Seth, the most ridiculously petty reason he could think of—control of a moderately successful midsize trucking company.

How could the job of running Davenport Trucking be

worth five murders and the wholesale destruction of Rachel's life? It made no sense, but it was the only logical motive Seth had been able to come up with after weeks of pondering the question.

What was he missing?

"If you go, I'm going with you," he said firmly.

She sent him a look of gratitude. "I'd appreciate that."

He looked down at his borrowed clothes. "I'd better change."

"Right." She waved toward a door to the right. "There's a bedroom behind that door. You can have it tonight."

He took his overnight bag into the bedroom and closed the door behind him. As he dressed, he took a moment to call Adam Brand for an update.

The FBI agent sounded harried when he answered. "Not the greatest time, Seth—"

"A lot's happened." He outlined the events of the day as economically as he could. "I'm about to go with Rachel to take a look at the body."

"This is bad." Brand didn't sound surprised, Seth noticed.

"But not unexpected?"

There was a brief pause on Brand's end of the line. "Not entirely."

"You're not going to tell me what you know, are you?"

"Not yet. Just keep an eye on Ms. Davenport and let me know everything that happens. I promise I'll tell you what I know as soon as I have all my ducks in a row on my end."

"I'm going to tell her I'm working for the FBI."

"No."

"I'm not comfortable lying to her."

"Seth, one of the reasons you've been so valuable to us is the fact that you're a damned good liar. Don't pretend you're suddenly a paragon of virtue. Just do what you do well and don't try to do my part of the job."

"I'm not going to keep lying to her," Seth insisted firmly. "I don't need your permission. I'm just giving you a little warning."

"You could screw things up badly if you tell her."

I could screw things up worse if I don't, he thought. "I'll tell her she has to be discreet. She'll understand. She can be trusted."

"If it gets around that the FBI is looking into some little stalker case in Bitterwood, Tennessee, it could screw up a very big, ongoing investigation."

"An investigation into what?"

"I can't tell you that." Brand had the decency to sound as if he regretted keeping Seth in the dark, at least. But Seth was losing patience with the skullduggery.

"Good night, Adam." He used Brand's first name deliberately. Adam Brand wasn't his boss, even if he paid the bills, and Seth would be damned if he'd kowtow to the man.

He hung up and tucked his phone in his back pocket. Out in the front room, he found Rachel at the window, her forehead pressed against the windowpane. At the sound of his footsteps, she turned to look at him. She'd been crying, though her eyes were mostly dry now.

Forgetting his promise to keep his distance, he crossed to where she stood, wrapping her up in a fierce hug. She stood stiff for a second before she relaxed in his arms, her cheek against his collarbone. Her arms curled around his waist, pulling him closer.

"Tell me I can do this," she said.

He wanted to tell her she didn't have to. But he'd seen the desperation in her eyes, the fierce need to be in control.

To be all right.

He released a slow, deep breath. "You can do this."

She nodded, her expression firming into iron-hard determination. "Let's go." She let go of him and walked slowly to the door, leaving him to follow.

Chapter Ten

She'd seen death twice in her life. First at the age of fifteen, when her mother's madness had led her to suicide. Some details were fuzzy in her memory but not all. Rachel still remembered the stark moment when she'd realized her mother had gone and wasn't coming back.

More recently, she'd watched her father die, a peaceful drift from slumber to utter stillness, protected from the cruelties of his life's end by the drugs his doctor had given him to make it easier to let go. They'd dulled his pain and given him a peace in death that his disease had denied him in life.

But until the moment the Sevier County morgue attendant pulled back the sheet on the battered body of Davis Rogers, she'd never seen death resulting from murder.

His face was battered almost beyond recognition, but the hourglass-shaped birthmark on his left biceps and the long white scar on his right knee filled in the blanks for her. It had been nearly seven years since she'd been in any kind of relationship with Davis, but he'd kept fit, the intervening years doing little to change the body she'd once known intimately.

Grief gouged a hole in her heart, and she turned away after nodding to the deputy sheriff who'd accompanied them into the morgue.

Seth stood just behind her, and it seemed as natural as breathing to walk into his arms when he reached out to her. He pulled her close for a moment before leading her out into the corridor, where the air seemed immediately lighter.

"I'm sorry," he murmured against her hair.

She wanted to cry, felt it burning its way into her chest, but she let it rise no further. She wasn't going to fall apart, especially not here in the midst of strangers like the deputy, who watched them both through narrowed eyes.

A few feet down the hallway, Antoine Parsons pushed away from the wall and crossed to where she, Seth and the deputy stood. "Is that the man you saw at Sequoyah House?" he asked Seth.

"Same clothes. Same condition." Seth moved his hand comfortingly up and down Rachel's back, but she felt tension gathering in him like a thunderstorm rising up a mountain. "I didn't think he had much of a chance of making it without help."

"We're still working on cause of death." The deputy, who'd introduced himself as John Mallory, seemed more interested in keeping his eye on Seth than meeting Antoine Parson's gaze. Seth himself seemed acutely aware of the deputy's scrutiny, though he tried not to show it.

He'd warned her, she thought. People looked at him differently because of who he was. What he'd been. And maybe if she'd never seen another side of him—the kind man, the brave protector—she'd be inclined to view him the same way.

She had viewed him with suspicion as recently as a few hours ago.

But that had been before he'd kissed her.

Was that all it took? Was that how easily she gave her trust?

She felt herself edging away from him, even as the thoughts roiled through her mind. He let go, let her move away, not looking at her as he did so. His gaze was fixed on John Mallory, his chin high and his mouth set with stubborn pride.

But even though he wasn't looking at her, she felt as if his defiant stance was meant for her as much as it was meant for the deputy. *This is who I am. This is what I deal with every day. If you can't handle it...*

"I'd like to request formal release of the body into the custody of the Bitterwood Police Department," Antoine said to Mallory. "Based on eyewitness testimony, we have reason to believe the assault leading to Davis Rogers's murder took place in the Bitterwood jurisdiction."

"Not so fast," Mallory said. "Until the C.O.D. is determined, the location of his death is still at issue."

"You really want this case?" Antoine argued. "You're about to have this man's family and their grief and questions crashing down on you. There's damned little evidence to go on, thanks to the rain and the removal of the body from the place where he was attacked. You're buying yourself a damned near unsolvable case, John."

"And you want it why, Antoine?"

"Because I think it may be connected to an open case in Bitterwood." Antoine flicked a quick look at Seth.

A slight twitch of Seth's eyes was his only response.

"I'll tell you what," Mallory said after a moment of consideration. "I'll talk to the sheriff, see if I can't get him to agree to a joint investigation, based on the testimony and pending the determination of the C.O.D. Then, if the cause of death suggests that the murder took place in the Bitterwood jurisdiction, we'll hand the whole thing over. Deal?"

Antoine didn't look happy, but he gave a nod. "I can live with that."

"Ms. Davenport gave us some information that should help us locate and inform Mr. Rogers's family of his death, so I'm going to go get the notifications started." Mallory shot Antoine a wry look. "Unless you'd like to handle that part of the investigation?"

Antoine smiled. "You found the body. You make the notifications."

Once Deputy Mallory was out of earshot, Antoine turned to Seth. "He really, really doesn't like you."

"I have that effect on a lot of people," Seth replied in a bone-dry tone. "I think in his case, it has more to do with Cleve Calhoun than with me. Cleve sucked Mallory's cousin into some land deal he's still holding a grudge about. Can't say I blame him. He lost a hell of a lot of money."

"If only he hadn't been so greedy, he could have avoided it?" Antoine asked. "Isn't that what you fellows say? Can't con an honest man?"

Seth slanted a look at Rachel, a hint of a smile curving his lips, though none of the amusement made it into his hard green eyes. "Something like that. I don't reckon that makes for much of an excuse, though."

"What happens now?" Rachel asked, finding the tense posturing between Seth and Antoine exhausting.

"Deputy Mallory will contact your friend's family. They'll make a formal identification for the record and, meanwhile, we'll get a warrant to search his room and his vehicle at Sequoyah House. I've already had it sealed off and posted a couple of officers at the bed-and-breakfast pending the warrant."

"Is there anything else we can do to help?"

Antoine looked at Seth. "If you could tell more about what you saw before you got hit on the head, we'd be better off. Maybe you saw the person who did it and you just don't remember."

Seth shook his head. "I doubt I'd be alive now if I'd seen who hit me." He glanced toward the door of the morgue. "Whoever did this doesn't seem interested in leaving witnesses behind."

"Witnesses to what?" Antoine asked.

Rachel wondered the same thing. What could Davis have seen that would warrant someone beating him to death? As far as she could tell, he'd come to town for her father's funeral. At most, he'd have been in Bitterwood for maybe a day before he was murdered.

The only thing he might have witnessed of any significance was what had happened to her at Smoky Joe's Saloon.

Which had to be the answer, Rachel realized.

"He was with me at Smoky Joe's Saloon last night," she said.

"I spoke to Joe Breslin earlier today," Seth explained as Antoine shot Rachel a curious look. "He told me he saw a man fitting Davis Rogers's description with Rachel last night at his bar. The man made a pass at Rachel, she rebuffed him and he left, according to Joe."

"Is that what his phone call was about?" Antoine asked. "The one you played for me?"

Seth looked at Rachel. "If he left before you did, what could he have possibly seen?"

"You think you were drugged." Antoine also looked at her. "Could Rogers have done it?"

She shook her head. "He wouldn't do that to me."

"It's been a few years since you were together," Seth

pointed out. "Maybe someone flashed a little cash at him—"

"He's a plaintiff's lawyer in Richmond and has done very well for himself. You saw where he was staying. Sequoyah House isn't cheap."

"Maybe he still holds a grudge about your breakup," Antoine suggested.

"He broke up with me," she answered bluntly. "I mean, it was mutual—we had both realized by then that we just wanted different things in life. But he was the one who finally made the move to end it. He's never tried to hurt me. You heard his message."

Her gut tightened as she realized the final call, the one she'd heard cut off with a thud, truly had been his last. At some point after that call had ended so abruptly, he'd been beaten to death.

Tears rose in her eyes, stinging hot. She blinked them back, but they kept coming, rolling down her cheeks in a sudden, unstoppable flood.

Seth's hands closed over her shoulders, warm and strong. It would be so easy to lean back against him, let herself melt in his solid heat.

But once she started depending on him, it might be difficult to stop. And he'd already made it clear that he wasn't in the market for any sort of entanglement.

"I'd like to borrow your phone again," Antoine said suddenly. "I'd like to record those last messages to you, if that's okay. Should have done it earlier. I could get a warrant, but this would be faster."

"Of course." She handed over her phone.

"I'll get it back to you as soon as I'm done. If you'd like to come to the station with me, I can record while you wait."

"Why don't we get something to eat?" Seth suggested.

"Ledbetter's Café is just around the corner." He looked up at Antoine. "Want us to bring you something?"

Antoine looked surprised by the offer. "Yeah. Sure. A pulled pork sandwich and some of Maisey's sweet potato fries." He pulled his wallet from the inside pocket of his jacket and handed Seth a ten, his eyes glinting with amusement. "You really are good at getting people to hand over their hard-earned money, aren't you, Hammond?"

Seth grinned back. "At least this time, you'll get a sandwich and fries out of it."

AFTER THE TRIP to the morgue, Rachel didn't have any appetite, but she let Seth cajole her into an omelet on toast. She managed to eat most of it, even though it seemed to stick in her throat. She sat back finally and watched Seth work his way through a plateful of barbecue ribs and Maisey Ledbetter's homemade slaw.

He ate with gusto, she noticed, like a man who appreciated a good, hot meal when one came his way. Even now, there was a hungry look about Seth Hammond that made her wonder how many times he'd been uncertain where his next meal would come from.

Seth ordered Antoine's barbecue plate as they got ready to leave, adding a slice of lemon meringue pie with a few dollars of his own money. At Rachel's questioning look, he shot her a sheepish grin. "I stole his pie at lunch one day in high school. He never knew who did it, but since I'm in the making-amends business these days—"

"Nice of you."

"Nice would have been if I hadn't nicked his pie in the first place."

Antoine raised an eyebrow at the unexpected slice of pie but thanked them and traded Rachel's cell phone for the food. He also had some information from the crime scene unit at Rachel's house. "They went over the place pretty thoroughly, but other than the piece of plastic and the shoe box you found, they couldn't find anything else of interest."

"What about the blood?"

"Not human. Animal of some kind, which wouldn't be hard to come by in a farming community like this."

She felt a rush of relief. "Thanks for checking."

"You're free to go back to your house, but if I were you, I'd change the locks as soon as you can. And put an alarm system in place."

"I'll definitely do that."

"I wish we had the manpower to send patrols by your house regularly, but we're already stretched pretty thin with a detective on leave and another recently retiring—"

"I understand," she said quickly, aware she was luckier than most people in her position. She could afford to hire protection if she needed it. Most people couldn't.

"I'm not going to ignore what's happening to you." Antoine's voice softened with concern. "I know this is the fifth murder connected to whatever's going on with you, and I won't avert my eyes and pretend it's not happening. I'm going to do my damnedest to figure out who's behind it."

"We've had some thoughts about that," Seth told him. He glanced at Rachel as if seeking permission to say anything further.

She gave a nod.

"The best I can tell, everything started about nine weeks ago, right?" Seth looked around the bull pen, his expression wary. "Is there someplace a little less open where we can discuss this?"

Antoine seemed surprised by the question, but he led

them down the hall to a small room equipped with a table, three chairs and a video camera mounted high in one corner. He showed them the button on the wall that controlled the camera. "It's off."

Seth looked at it closely, then took the lone chair on the far side of the table, leaving Rachel and Antoine to sit in the other two. "Sorry if I'm coming across paranoid, but I'm not sure who to trust these days."

Antoine shot him a wry look. "Tell me about it."

Rachel frowned. "What does that mean?"

"Are you suggesting there's someone on the police force involved with what's happening to Rachel?" Seth asked.

"I don't know. I don't have any particular reason to think so, but I have reservations about the way some things are done around here. I'm just saying I understand Hammond's caution."

"I'm wary of anyone with a badge," Seth said wryly. "Though a lot of that's my own damned fault."

"Too bad. We're having all kinds of trouble with fraud cases these days, the economy being what it is." Antoine sighed. "There are just too many ways to part good folks from their hard-earned money, and it wouldn't hurt to have an insider on our side."

"I'm wondering if money isn't the driving force behind what's going on at Davenport Trucking," Seth said.

Rachel looked at him, surprised. "We're pretty successful, I'll grant you, but I'm not sure we're five murders worth of successful."

"You'd be surprised how cheaply murder can be bought," Antoine muttered.

Seth twined his fingers on the table in front of him, the muscles and tendons flexing and unflexing, drawing

Rachel's gaze. A couple of hours ago, those hands had been on her. Touching her. Branding her.

She swallowed with difficulty.

"You said you think it started nine weeks ago?" Antoine nudged.

Rachel realized Seth's gaze was on her, green eyes blazing with awareness, as if he'd been reading her thoughts. She flushed.

"With the first murder. April Billings. Summer intern at Davenport Trucking. She'd just had her going-away party at the office the day she was killed. Remember?"

Rachel nodded, pain darting through her chest. "She was so excited to be going back to college. She had missed all her friends over the summer, and she had managed to get into a really popular class in her major that she was looking forward to attending." She blinked hard, fighting tears at the memory. "She made me want to go back to college all over again."

"You were close to her?" Antoine asked.

"Yeah. I guess she gravitated to me because I'm a librarian. I mean, I was. That was what she wanted to be, too. And she'd have been a good one." Rachel dashed away a tear that had slipped free of her control. "I really wanted that for her."

Seth's gaze softened. "She was a nice girl. She should've had that life she wanted."

"Who knew that you and April were friends?" Antoine asked Rachel.

"Anybody who worked there knew," Seth answered for her. "Rachel is big news around the company. Even the guys in the garage were speculating what it meant that Mr. Davenport had clearly brought her on to be his successor."

"You were?" Rachel hadn't realized.

"Well, sure. You'll be the boss. We aren't sure if you plan to keep running the place the way your daddy did or if you'll change things around." There were secrets in his green eyes but also amusement. Rachel realized there were things he could tell her—wanted to tell her—but not until they were alone.

That realization—that shock of intimacy—made her feel warm all over.

"Was anyone hostile to the idea?" Antoine asked.

Seth gave a quick shake of his head. "Worried, maybe. Jobs can be hard to come by these days. People feel lucky to be employed, and anything that threatens to change things—"

"But surely they knew the company was doing well, even with my father's illness," Rachel protested. "He worked hard to make everyone feel comfortable and secure with what was happening."

"It's easy to feel secure when you're not one paycheck away from ruin."

Even though she knew Seth didn't mean his words as a rebuke, they still stung a little. Because he was right. She'd never had to worry where her next meal would come from. Or whether or not she'd be able to make the next mortgage payment or pay the next utility bill.

"I still don't see how those worries constitute a motive for murder," she said more sharply than she'd intended.

"No," Seth agreed. "What's happening here is too personal."

"You mean this is all about hurting Ms. Davenport?" Antoine sounded skeptical, to Rachel's relief. Because the idea that someone hated her enough to kill people to torment her was utterly horrifying.

"Not that exactly," Seth said with a quick shake of his head. "But I do think that whoever's doing this knows enough about her life and her history to choose his actions to injure her in the worst possible way."

He knows, she realized, recognizing the hint of pity in Seth's eyes. *He knows about the missing year.*

But how? How could he know? Almost nobody outside of the clinic in North Carolina knew how she'd spent the year following her mother's death. Her father had told everyone that she'd gone to school abroad to get away from the aftermath of her mother's suicide, and nobody had questioned it because nobody but her father had seen the state she was in that night. He'd taken quick steps to protect her.

How could any of this be about what had happened fifteen years ago? How was that even possible?

"But what's the point?" Antoine asked. "What does hurting Ms. Davenport this way accomplish?"

"It could drive her out of the CEO position at Davenport Trucking," Seth suggested.

Rachel shook her head. "We don't pull in those kinds of profits. Sure, we do well. People get paid, and we make a comfortable profit. I'm not hurting for money. But no way are all these murders about taking over Davenport Trucking. There's no upside."

For the first time, Seth looked doubtful. "It's the only thing so far that's even close to answering all of the questions."

"Why not just kill me, then? Why torment me instead?"

"If you're killed now, what happens to the company?" Antoine asked. "Who gets your shares?"

"My mother's brother. Rafe. He owns about twenty percent of the company already because he put up seed money when the company started. But Uncle Rafe doesn't want to run the company. My father even offered the job to him before he brought me into the picture, and Uncle Rafe said no. He's a musician and a promoter."

"We need to find out what happens if you're still alive but unable to run the company," Seth said quietly. "It seems to be the point of trying to drive you crazy, and that appears to be what's going on here."

"I told you, I don't know. I've never asked that question." Maybe she should have, she realized, given her history.

"Who *would* know?" Antoine suddenly looked interested.

"My father's personal lawyer, of course. Maybe my stepmother, Diane—but she's out of town. It's possible he'd have told Garrett McKenzie—

"Former mayor Garrett McKenzie?" Antoine whistled softly.

"Old family friend." She had never felt self-conscious about her family connections before, but both Antoine and Seth were making her feel like a pampered princess with their reactions.

Was that fair? Was she supposed to feel ashamed of having a father who had worked hard and provided well for his family?

"Anybody else?" Seth asked.

"The lawyer for sure. I'm not positive about Diane or anyone else." She risked another quick look at Seth, trying to read his expression. But he was suddenly closed off, impossible to read.

Just when she most needed to know what he was thinking.

Chapter Eleven

The house was midnight quiet, even with all the lights blazing. Rachel had wanted to return to her father's house to spend the night rather than the cabin. There'd been a look of stubborn determination in her eyes when she'd told him her decision. They'd stopped to get their things at the cabin and arrived just as the grandfather clock in the den was chiming twelve.

Rachel watched him carry their bags inside with a look of apology in her weary eyes. "I know you think I'm crazy to come back here. But I won't be run out of my house. Not by the son of a bitch who's doing this."

He admired her determination, even if he'd prefer to stash her somewhere safer. "Understood."

"I must be taxing your patience."

"Oh, not for a few days yet."

The teasing reply earned him a tired smile. "You're a trouper."

"So are you."

Her response was another quick smile and a shake of her head as she dropped her car keys on the entry table and kicked off her shoes.

"You need sleep," he told her. "Go on up to bed. I'll lock up."

She caught his arm as he turned toward the door.

"How do you know about the time I spent in Westminster?"

He considered pretending he didn't know what she was talking about. But she deserved better than to be treated like a child. "Is that where you were? Is it a hospital?"

She took a small step back, her hand falling from his arm. "You don't know?"

Great. Now she thought he'd tricked her. "I didn't know the details. I just guessed the situation."

Her lips pressed into a thin line. "I can see why you were so good at what you used to do. You're really kind of spooky."

"I guessed about Westminster because it was the only thing that would explain the elaborate ruse in the attic."

Her brow lifted. "Restaging the moment of my big meltdown?"

"You were really shaken by what you saw. I could tell you were beginning to doubt yourself when we didn't find the evidence you expected right away."

She closed her eyes, as if she could blot out the memory of those moments. "I used to relive that night. Over and over again. Trying to stop it. Trying to reach her before she pulled the trigger. I went almost three months with no more than an hour or two of undisturbed sleep each night. I came really close to dying because of it. I couldn't eat. I lost a lot of weight. Couldn't think straight. All I could do was remember something I couldn't change, no matter how hard I tried."

He brushed his fingers against her face, unable to stop himself. She leaned into his touch, her face lifting even as she kept her eyes tightly shut. He brushed his lips against her furrowed brow. "I'm sorry."

She rested her head against his chest. "She wanted me to die with her."

His heart contracted. "She tried to kill you?"

She shook her head quickly. "Remember that window in the attic, the one by the trapdoor? When I got up to the attic, that window was open. The wind was blowing outside, whipping the curtains around. She told me she'd opened it for me. Because she knew how much I wanted to fly."

Seth closed his eyes, remembering Rachel's drug-induced words on the bridge. *She said I should fly.*

"I was fifteen going on thirty. I wanted to be grown, to be my own woman. When she was lucid, that idea seemed to terrify her. But when she was drowning in madness, she told me to fly."

He hugged her close. "I'm sorry."

"For a long time I couldn't remember much of it at all. I was terrified people were hiding things from me about her death, that I'd done something to hurt her."

"My God."

"Most of the memories came back on their own. And I knew what I didn't want to remember." She looked up at him with hard, shiny eyes. "There was a moment, right after she pulled the trigger and was lying there, bleeding all over that drop cloth, that the thought of flight seemed so sweet, so tempting. I remember, I walked past her body to the open window and stared down at the patio below. Those flagstones looked hard. Unforgiving. But it would be over in a flash, and then the pain would be gone."

He pressed his lips to her forehead again, swallowing the horror swirling in his chest at her words.

"I'm terrified of heights now. Just climbing the ladder into the attic scared the hell out of me. I think it comes from the memory of standing at that window, staring down at my own death."

He stroked her hair, hating her mother for doing such

a thing to her. "How many people know about Westminster?"

She looked up at him. "Almost nobody. My father came up with an elaborate story about my going to live with a great-aunt in England and going to school there. All my old friends didn't know what to say to a girl whose mother had killed herself, so it wasn't much trouble to discourage them from trying to reach me."

"I've never heard a word about it, and you know what a gossip mill this town can be."

"I've wondered whether my father was protecting himself as much as he was protecting me. From the stigma of having a mentally ill daughter as well as a wife who committed suicide." She looked shamed by the admission. "I shouldn't have said that. I know he was protecting me. And he didn't see me as mentally ill now or he wouldn't have left the business to me."

"And nobody else knew?"

"Well, my great-aunt in England knew, because she had to be the alibi. Uncle Rafe and Aunt Janeane—they live in Bryson City, near Winchester. My doctors and nurses at the clinic. My father, of course." She crossed her arms over her body, rubbing her arms as if she was cold.

Seth pulled off his denim jacket and wrapped it around her. "Better?"

The smoldering gaze she lifted to meet his almost made his knees buckle. "Thank you."

Get your mind on the stalker. Think about the kind of payback you want against him.

The ideas for revenge flooding his head helped cool his ardor, along with a slight step backward to take him out of the immediate impact of her delicate scent and sad-eyed vulnerability. "What about the trustees of your father's business? Would any of them know?"

"I don't think so. Well, maybe my stepmother. She's always treated me as if I'm a little fragile." Her brow creased again. "A lot of people do when they know my mother committed suicide."

"It's a trauma most people can't imagine."

"I hope they never have reason to know what it feels like." She shivered. "You don't suspect Diane, do you?"

Thanks to Mark Bramlett's final words, they knew the person who'd hired him to commit the first four murders had been a man. But Diane Davenport could have hired someone to do all the dirty work for her, he supposed. Even the solicitation. "How much would she stand to gain if you were removed as CEO?"

"As far as I know, nothing more than she'd gain if I remained CEO. That's something I need to ask my father's lawyer in the morning."

Seth wondered if he'd be able to turn off his mind tonight long enough to get some much-needed sleep. While logic told him it wasn't likely the intruder from earlier that day would repeat an invasion so soon after the police had scoured the place for evidence, instinct told him he needed to stay on full alert.

"Maybe I should sleep down here on the sofa," he suggested.

Her cheeks flushed pink as she smiled. "I'm way too tired to make any moves on you tonight. Your virtue is safe with me."

He smiled at her attempt to lighten the mood. "I appreciate that, but I was actually thinking about the best way to keep you safe."

Her smile faded. "From intruders?"

"I don't think it's likely anyone will try anything tonight, after all the police presence today, but my gut says better safe than sorry."

"You listen to your gut a lot?" The question was serious.

"I do."

She slowly walked toward him, closing the distance between them. He found himself unable to back away, frozen in place by the desire in her eyes. She laid her hand in the middle of his chest and let it slide slowly down to the flat of his stomach. "What does your gut tell you to do with me?"

He couldn't stop a dry laugh from spilling from his throat. "I don't think that's my gut talkin', sugar."

Her eyes widened slightly, then she laughed, the sound belly deep. It was a glorious sound, he thought. Rich and deep and utterly sane. If he'd harbored a doubt about her mental stability, that laugh crushed it to powder.

"I like you, Seth Hammond. I hope like hell you decide to stick around once this is all over." She rose to her tiptoes and pressed her mouth to his, the kiss light and undemanding.

It nearly unraveled him anyway. His whole body trembled as he watched her walk away, up the stairs and out of sight.

SETH DIDN'T LOOK as if he'd gotten much sleep when he greeted Rachel the next morning with a cup of hot coffee and a creditable omelet. "I think you should call the company lawyer as soon as his office opens. See if he can work us in this morning."

She took the omelet and cup of coffee to the small table in the kitchen nook, "Got our agenda all worked out for today, have you?"

"The sooner we figure this out, the better," he said firmly.

The sooner you get to leave, you mean, she thought

with a hint of morning-after bleakness. All her confidence of the night before had faded into doubts by the time she'd drifted to sleep. At least her subconscious had been certain of his ability to keep her safe. If she'd dreamed at all last night, she couldn't remember it and it hadn't disturbed her sleep.

She called the lawyer as soon as his office opened and he agreed to see her right away if she could get there before nine. His office was in Maryville, about twenty minutes away, but fortunately she'd showered and dressed before making the call, so they reached Maryville with time to spare.

"Am I going to be forced to fire you for ditching work?" she asked lightly as they passed the big Davenport Trucking sign on West Sperry Road.

"I took vacation days. Cleared it with your stepbrother before I went looking for Davis Rogers."

"Very conscientious."

"What about your stepbrother?" he asked with a sideways glance toward her. "If you were incapacitated, could he take over as the CEO?"

"I don't think he wants to be CEO. His passion is hospitality. He used to work at a big resort on the Mississippi Gulf Coast before things went bad down that way and a lot of people were laid off. I think he's still hoping to get back into that line of work someday. I think he's only stayed at Davenport Trucking this long because his mother married my father. I won't be surprised if he gives me his notice sooner rather than later."

"Okay." Seth fell silent until they reached Ed Blount's office in the Maryville downtown area. The lawyer's office was located in an old two-story white clapboard house converted to upstairs and downstairs offices. Blount's suite was on the lower floor, and he greeted

Rachel with an affectionate kiss on the cheek and a look of puzzlement.

"I didn't expect to see you this soon," Ed told her. "If you're here about the will reading—"

"It's not that," she said quickly. "I do have a question about my father's business, though."

"Okay." Ed spotted Seth, his sandy eyebrows lifting.

"Ed, this is Seth Hammond. Seth, Ed Blount."

Seth's face was a mask. "We've met."

From the look on the lawyer's face, it must not have been a pleasant acquaintance. "What is he doing here?"

"I can go," Seth said.

"No." She caught his wrist, holding him in place. She turned back to Ed. "Let's just stipulate that Seth was no doubt a complete ass in the past, and you have every right to distrust him for whatever it was he did to you—"

"It wasn't to him," Seth said. "It was his daughter."

She shot him a look. He met her gaze, unflinching for a moment. Then his eyes dropped, and he turned his head away.

"She thought you loved her," Ed growled.

"I know."

"That's it? You know?"

Seth's gaze lifted slowly. "I could tell you that I regret it, but you're not going to believe me, and it won't make her feel a damned bit better."

"What about her college money? Can you give that back to her?"

Rachel's heart sank painfully at the look of shame on Seth's face. But he didn't look away from Ed. "I tried."

Ed stared at him. "When?"

"About a year ago. She shoved it back to me and told me she didn't want my dirty money."

"Where is it now?"

"I gave it to the soup kitchen in Knoxville. I know Lauren used to volunteer there."

"That's where she met you," Ed snarled. "You played on her soft heart and convinced her you were just down on your luck and looking for someone to believe in you."

Seth's expression grew stony. His voice, when he spoke, was dry and uninflected. "I did."

"You broke her heart."

"I know."

"I'm sick of hearing that!" he bellowed, charging toward Seth.

"Ed." Rachel grabbed the lawyer's arm and put herself between him and Seth, struggling to keep a sudden tremor in her knees from spreading to the rest of her limbs. "You had to work me in and I don't want to run out of time because of this."

"I'll wait outside." Seth exited abruptly, closing the door behind him, leaving Rachel alone with Ed.

The lawyer glared with loathing at the closed door, his breathing coming in short, harsh grunts. "What the hell are you doing with that man?"

"It's a long story. And it's not relevant to what I'm here to find out."

Ed stared at her in consternation, visibly trying to collect himself. Finally, in a calmer tone of voice, he asked, "What are you here to find out?"

She nudged him toward his office door, shooting an apologetic smile toward the pretty red-haired receptionist who had watched the whole debacle with her mouth in an O of surprise. "I need to know what would happen to Davenport Trucking if I were no longer able to act as CEO."

WELL, THAT *had gone well.*

Seth sank onto the top porch step and stared across the tree-shaded street at the mostly full parking lot of a sprawling one-story medical clinic. Pediatrics, he realized as the cars came and went with their cargo of harried moms and coughing, sniffling children.

Maybe he should write Rachel a note, leave it on her windshield and walk back to Davenport Trucking. He could hang around until lunchtime and see if one of the guys in the fleet garage could drive him to the rental car place in Alcoa in exchange for lunch.

But before he talked himself to his feet, the door opened behind him and Rachel stepped out, stopping short as she spotted him on the porch step. "Oh. I was halfway expecting you to be gone."

He rose and turned to face her, his spine rigid with a combination of shame and stubborn pride. "I was halfway to talking myself into going."

"You warned me," she said quietly, nodding toward the car.

"I did." He fell into step with her as they walked to the Honda.

"Didn't you realize who we were going to see?"

"I didn't connect the names." He forced a grim smile. "Lots of Blounts in Blount County, Tennessee."

"Did you really try to pay her back?"

He slanted a look at her, trying not to be hurt by the question. "Yes."

"And when she refused, you gave the money to the soup kitchen?"

"Foundations of Hope. Downtown. Ask for Dave Pelletier."

She paused with her key halfway to the ignition. "You always sound as if you're telling the truth."

"And you can't trust that I am." It wasn't a question. He saw the doubt in her eyes.

"I want to."

"That's not enough. You have to be sure, and you can't afford to let time and experience prove my motives are sincere."

"I don't know who to trust at all." She looked so afraid, and he hated himself for adding to her distress.

"Sometimes you just have to trust your instincts," he said quietly. "What do your instincts tell you?"

She lifted her gaze to meet his. "That you want to keep me safe."

A strange sensation, part agony, part joy, burned a hole in the center of his chest. "You're crazy."

Even though tears shined in her eyes, she laughed. "That's not a nice thing to say to a woman with my mental health history."

He laughed, too, even though he felt like crying, as well. "I won't hurt you. Not if there's anything I can do to avoid it. And if you ever begin to doubt me, you say so and I'll be gone."

"Deal." She held out her hand.

He shook it, his fingers tingling where hers touched him. He resisted the powerful urge to pull her into his arms and let go, turning to buckle himself in. "What now? What did you learn?"

"A lot. But I'm not sure how it's going to help us."

Chapter Twelve

"So the trustees choose the CEO?" Seth asked a few minutes later, after Rachel had summarized what Ed Blount had told her. "Is that the gist of it?"

Rachel nodded as she threaded her way through traffic on Lamar Alexander Parkway, heading toward the mountains. "There are parameters, of course. My father apparently left a list of approved candidates that the trustees have to choose from first. If none of those candidates is willing to take the job, the trustees are tasked with a circumscribed candidate search. My father apparently left detailed instructions."

"Blount wouldn't give you the details, though?"

"Not before the reading of the will next Tuesday...."

"But?" he prodded, apparently reading her hesitation.

"He mentioned that my uncle helped my father come up with the list. I think Uncle Rafe might be willing to tell me now if I ask him."

"So let's ask him."

She shot him a smile. "Where do you think we're heading?"

Her uncle lived across the state line in Bryson City, where he and his wife, Janeane, ran a music hall catering primarily to Smoky Mountains tourists. The drive from Maryville took over two hours, but Rachel couldn't complain much about the view as their route twisted through the Smokies, past bluffs cut into the earth and sweeping vistas of the mountains spreading north and east, their tips swallowed by lingering mists that even the sunny day had not completely dissipated.

They arrived at Song Valley Music Hall in time for lunch. The fall tourist season was just starting, which meant they didn't have their choice of tables when they walked into the dimly lit dining hall, but they didn't have to wait in line, either.

Uncle Rafe himself came out to greet them, menu in hand and a smile on his face. His eyes widened as he recognized her. "Rachel, my dolly! You should have called to let me know you were coming. I just gave away the last front-row table for the show!"

"That's okay—we'll enjoy it anyway." She gave her uncle a kiss and turned to Seth. He looked uncomfortable, which struck her as odd, considering his history as a con artist. Weren't con men chameleons? "Uncle Rafe, this is Seth Hammond, a friend of mine. Seth, this is my uncle Rafe Hunter."

Her uncle's blue eyes narrowed shrewdly. "Hammond."

Seth nodded. "Yes, sir."

"Any kin to Delbert Hammond?"

Seth's expression froze in place. "My father."

Uncle Rafe nodded slowly. "There's a resemblance."

Seth's mask slipped a bit, revealing dismay in his green eyes. "So I'm told."

Rafe cocked his head to one side. "You're the one got burned."

Rachel looked from her uncle to Seth. His left hand rose and settled against his right shoulder, kneading the skin through his shirt. "That's right. Long time ago."

"Heard you've been playing nursemaid to Cleve Calhoun for the last little while. That true?"

"Yes, sir." Seth's hand dropped away from his shoulder. "He's at a rehab place now, though. His son talked him into giving it a go."

"You couldn't get him to agree?"

"Don't reckon I tried, really. I've never had any luck talking Cleve into much of anything.

Uncle Rafe smiled a little at Seth's admission. "I'll buy that. You still in the life?"

"Uncle Rafe—"

"I am not," Seth answered.

"You sure?" Her uncle's gaze went from Seth's stony face to Rachel's.

"I've found there's no long-term job satisfaction in lying to people for a living."

Uncle Rafe's gaze swept back to meet Seth's. "I don't know, son. I'm a showman, and what is that but lying to people for a living? Putting on an act, sucking them into a narrative of my choosing?"

"The people at a show know what they're seeing isn't real," Seth answered slowly. "They're willing participants in their own deception."

Uncle Rafe's well-lined face creased with a smile. "Damn good answer, boy." He hooked his arm through Rachel's and led her to the second row of tables facing the large stage. "Gotta go start deceiving this room full of willing participants in their own deception," he said with a wink in Seth's direction. "You'll stick around after the show, of course?"

"Absolutely," Rachel agreed. "I need to ask you a few questions about the trucking company. Will you have time between lunch and dinner?"

"I'll make time, dolly girl." He gave her a quick kiss and headed for the back of the restaurant.

The food at her uncle's place was good, simple home cooking. Janeane ran the kitchen, while he booked the acts and kept the daily shows going, varying things up every few weeks to keep it fresh for returning customers, Rachel told Seth while they were waiting for their orders. "Probably sixty to seventy percent of their customers are tourists," she added. "But they get a lot of locals, too, who like to take in a show. He brings in a lot of young, upcoming bluegrass and country performers. He has a real talent for knowing who's going to be the next big thing."

"You're proud of him," Seth said with a smile.

"Yeah, I am."

His smile shifted slightly. "Nice to have someone to be proud of."

"You don't?"

"There's Dee. She's the real star of the family." Rachel could tell from the look in his eyes that he thought the world of his sister. "I knew when we were little she was going to be special. She never let anything that was going on around us faze her. She knew what she wanted, and she went after it. And she always did it the right way. No shortcuts. No stomping all over someone else to get ahead. I used to think my parents must have stolen her from some nice family, 'cause she wasn't a damned thing like the rest of us."

"Are you two close?"

The pain she occasionally glimpsed in his eyes was back. "No. My fault. I wore out my welcome with Delilah a long time ago."

"She helped you out with me."

He reached across the table, lightly tapping the back of her hand. "That was for you, sugar. Not for me."

"She doesn't believe you've changed?"

A mask of indifference came over his face. "Nobody does."

"I do," she said without thinking.

His gaze focused on hers, green eyes blazing. "You don't know me, Rachel. And most of what you've heard and seen should scare the hell out of you. Don't make up some fantasy about the misunderstood tough guy who just needs someone to care. I'm not misunderstood. People understand exactly who I was. I've earned their disgust."

"You're not pulling con jobs anymore—"

"So? I did. I did them willingly, with skill and determination."

"And then you stopped."

He shook his head. "Because I finally disgusted even myself! Do you understand what I did?"

She found herself floundering for an answer. "You lied to people and conned them out of money—"

"I hurt people," he said in a low, hard growl. "Not with a gun or a knife but with my lies. Do you know Lauren Blount, Rachel?"

She shook her head. "Not really."

"When I met her, she was nineteen. Pretty as a postcard and as sweet as Carolina honey. I convinced her I wanted a life with her, but because of my meth-dealing daddy and how he blew up my whole family, I couldn't catch a break. Showed her my burn scars, told her how I got them saving my mama from the burning house after my daddy nearly killed us all."

"Is that really what happened? That's what Uncle

Rafe was talking about earlier, right? About your getting burned."

He met her gaze. "So what if it was? That's what con men do, don't you get it? We take the truth and use it to sell our lies. I had burn scars from draggin' my mama out of that house 'cause she was too drunk to get out herself, and yeah, it makes a real pitiful story. Women see your scars, get all soft and gooey about how you're some hero, and they don't even see you're playing them like fiddles."

She looked away, feeling ill.

"I had Lauren eating out of my hand. I told her I had this idea for a business, see, and I needed some seed money, but no banks or businesspeople were going to take a chance on some old hillbilly like me. I made it sound like a sure thing. I made it sound like our future. And she ate it up. She saw the poor sad sack who just needed a good woman's love to make things okay for him, and she went for the bait in a heartbeat. Just like I knew she would."

"Then what did you do?"

"She gave me the money she'd saved up for her next two semesters of college. Cried a little as she did it, telling me that even if nobody else believed in me, she did."

Tears burned Rachel's eyes as she tried to picture herself in Lauren Blount's situation. Madly in love and wanting so much to help him out. Would she have given him the money?

She didn't think she liked the answer.

"I took the money and I left town. Left her a note telling her that she needs to be careful about who she trusts in the future." He smiled, but it was a horrible sight, full of anger and self-loathing. "She's taken that warning to heart. I don't think she trusts anyone anymore."

Silence fell between them. Finally, Rachel found the courage to speak. "Didn't she press charges against you?"

He shook his head. "She gave me the money willingly, and I was vague about what I planned to do with it. She would have had to try to prove her case in court, and she didn't want to face that kind of scrutiny." He grimace-smiled again. "Lucky me."

"My God."

His green eyes flashed at her again. "Now you're getting it."

She felt sick. "What made you quit the con game?"

"Cleve's stroke."

She narrowed her eyes. "Really."

"He was helpless for a long while. His own son didn't want to hear from him. He had no one in the world to take care of him but me. I realized I didn't want to give up even part of my life for the old bastard. What had he ever done for me but turn me into a criminal?"

"Why did you help him, then?"

"Because there was no one else. Someone had to."

"It could have been the state. Or he could have hired a caretaker. It didn't have to be you."

"It did." He looked down at the flatware bundle wrapped up in a slip of paper by his elbow. He pulled the flatware to him and began to play with the bundle, turning it slowly in a circle as if he needed time to organize his thoughts. After a minute, he pushed it aside and looked up at her. "It took a day or two, but I remembered that Cleve had taken me in when I had no one else. Everybody turned on my family, and especially me, because they all knew I was going to turn out like my daddy anyway. Why bother?"

"What about your mother? Couldn't she have helped you?"

"My mama is a drunk. Has been since I was a kid because it was the only way she could keep livin' with a man who beat her up for fun."

Rachel covered her mouth in dismay.

"Tawdry, ain't it?" He'd slipped easily back into the hard mountain twang of his raising. "That's the Hammonds of Smoky Ridge for you."

"What do you think would have happened if Cleve hadn't taken an interest in you?"

"I'd be in jail. Maybe even hooked on meth. Maybe dead."

"Cleve saved you from that."

"And introduced me to a life that seemed like a no-brainer at the time. I could lie with the best of them. I'd been lyin' all my life, coverin' up for what happened in that house." His lips curved slightly, but his gaze seemed focused somewhere far away. "It was so easy."

"Until it wasn't."

His gaze snapped back to hers. "You know what con men really do, Rachel? They kill your soul. You start out a normal person. Caring. Trusting. And then he strikes, and you're never the same. You trust no one. Nothing. You're afraid to be nice, because it makes you vulnerable. You're afraid to care because it makes you an easy mark. You meet a nice guy, a good guy, a guy who would treat you right, and you can't let yourself believe him because you know sweet words and a tender touch can hide a monster." He leaned toward her, his gaze so intense it made her stomach quiver. "That's what I did to Lauren Blount. It's what I did to God knows how many people along the way."

She didn't know what to say. She didn't even know what to feel.

"I did that." He sat back, looking away. "I don't know

how a man can forgive himself for that. I don't know how he lives with it. He can try to pay back the money, he can promise he'll never do anything like that again, but he can't change the fact that he had that kind of evil inside him and he let it have free rein. How do I live with that?"

She had no answer. The things he'd told her, the things he'd described, sickened her. Yet, the obvious guilt and remorse he felt touched her heart, as well. He'd been young and desperate, and while he was right—those facts weren't excuses for the things he'd done—they were, at least, mitigating factors.

At thirty, was Seth Hammond the same man he'd been at twenty? Obviously not. But was she crazy to take a chance on a man who'd lived the kind of life he had?

The food came, but she'd long since lost her appetite. Seth toyed with his food as well, eating little. He seemed determined not to look at her for the rest of the time, and it was a relief when the music started, giving them both somewhere to park their reluctant gazes for a while.

Uncle Rafe came back to their table after the music set was over and looked with dismay at their barely touched plates. "Didn't like the food?"

"My fault," Seth said quietly. "I brought up a stomach-turning topic just as the food arrived."

Uncle Rafe's eyes narrowed as he waved over a waitress and asked her to put the food in a couple of to-go boxes. "Take it with you. Maybe you'll be hungry later. Now. What was it that you needed to ask me about the trucking company?"

"This is going to sound like an odd question, but it's important. When Dad came to you to discuss his will, he asked you to help him make up a roster of preapproved candidates for the job of CEO if I were unable to fulfill my duties. I asked Ed Blount to give me the list, but he won't do it before the will reading next week. I need to see the list now."

"Goodness, girl, whatever for? You're the CEO, free and clear, so what does the list matter now?"

"Someone may be trying to change the situation," she said quietly.

Uncle Rafe leaned closer. "Change the situation how?"

Rachel glanced at Seth. He was looking at her, finally, his gaze intense. He gave a little nod, and she lifted her chin and met her uncle's troubled gaze. "I think someone's trying to drive me crazy."

Chapter Thirteen

The Song Valley Music Hall's office was a small room in the back of the building, nestled between the large kitchen and the public restrooms. The decor was strictly old-fashioned country charm, but Seth was relieved to see that whatever his eccentricities, Rafe Hunter took his business seriously. A new computer with a flat screen monitor and an all-in-one printer/copier sat in one corner. Shiny steel file cabinets took up one wall, while a well-organized storage cubby occupied the other.

Rafe went straight to the computer and called up a document file. At a glance—all Seth got before Rafe sent the file to print and closed it up—there were six names on the list. "Do any of those people know Mr. Davenport was considering them as possible CEOs?" he asked.

"I believe George let them know. He wouldn't want to give the trustees a list of people unwilling to consider the job, after all."

The paper came out of the printer, and Rafe plucked it up and handed it to Rachel. "There's your list. I hope to God you're wrong about your suspicions, dolly. Maybe you should come stay here with Janeane and me for a while."

"It's not a bad idea." Seth tamped down the part of him that was begging her to tell her uncle no. It made sense for her to get out of Bitterwood for a while. She could let Seth look into that list of people while she stayed safely out of it.

Safely away from him, too.

"No," she said, and part of him nearly wilted with relief. "This is my life we're talking about. I'm tired of letting everyone else make decisions for me. I need to be part of ending this mess."

"Are you rethinking your decision to be the company CEO?" Rafe gave his niece a probing look.

"I don't know," she said finally. "I never thought I wanted to take over the company permanently, but I love the people there and I want the company to be a success. My dad believed I was the person who could do it, and the more time I've spent there over the past year, the more convinced I am that he's right. I can do this job. I can do it well and take care of our customers and our employees. And I really want to, at least for a while longer. I can always go back to being a librarian later."

Rafe cupped her cheek with one big hand. "Why don't you tell me what's been going on?"

As Rachel related the things that had happened around her for the past two months, Seth found himself watching Rafe carefully for his reaction. Could he have his own reasons for wanting control of the company? The music hall seemed to be successful, but appearances could be deceiving, as Seth well knew. Rafe could be neck-deep in debt. He might be a compulsive gambler or have a bad drug habit that sucked his profits dry.

It might have been too obvious to kill Rachel before her father's death, since Rafe would be the prime suspect. He was at the top of the list to get control of the company if she were dead. Which would also make him the prime suspect if her death was suspicious in any way.

But if she were unable to fulfill the requirements of the job due to mental health problems, Rafe would have a great deal of influence if he wanted it, and nobody would suspect he'd engineered the situation.

He'd helped create this list of people to take her place. Might he have taken an even greater role, as her closest living relative, if she were declared incompetent?

If he harbored such wicked thoughts, they certainly didn't show in his horrified expression as he listened to Rachel's story. "My God, you should have called your aunt Janeane and me for help."

"I wasn't sure what was going on," she admitted. "If Seth hadn't found me on that bridge, I don't even know if I'd be alive."

Rafe blanched, his hand shaking as he lifted it to her face again. "Who would do such a thing to you?"

"I don't know."

"We think it must have something to do with Davenport Trucking," Seth said. "That's why we need the list."

Rafe's gaze snapped up to meet his. "What is your part in all this?"

The easy answer, of course, was that FBI Special Agent in Charge Adam Brand had asked him to keep an eye on Rachel. But since he hadn't shared that information with her yet, he didn't think it was a good idea to spill the beans in front of her uncle.

"I work at Davenport Trucking," he answered. "The family's been good to me, and I know a little something about deception. I guess in some ways, I'm uniquely suited to unravel a plot against Rachel."

"Thank you kindly for your help, then. But I can take care of her now. Dolly, you need to pack up and come stay with Janeane and me."

"No." Rachel's response was quiet but firm. "I'm an adult, and I will take care of myself."

"Rachel—" Seth began.

She turned her cool blue gaze to him. "Yes?"

He didn't want to argue with her in front of her uncle, so he nodded toward the list. "Anything stand out?"

She took a look at the list, her brow furrowed. "Not really. Most of the people are Davenport Trucking employees—Stan Alvis, who's the chief financial officer, Drayton Lewis, our comptroller, your direct supervisor at the garage, Gary Adams—hmm." She frowned a little.

"What?" Seth asked.

"Paul is on this list." She looked up at her uncle. "If he was willing to be CEO, why didn't my dad give him the job outright?"

Rafe shrugged. "He wanted it to be you. In fact, I'm the one who suggested Paul. I figured Diane would be hurt if we didn't, and the boy has been a loyal employee for nearly a decade now."

Seth considered what he knew about Paul Bailey. The guy came across as a put-together, confident business-man, but even though he'd been with the company for years, he didn't haunt the doors of the place the way George Davenport had, or even some of the other people on the short list. Seth's own boss, Gary, worked long hours and was a stickler about getting the job done right. He was blue-collar and rednecked, but Gary was smart, too. What he lacked in formal education, he made up for with his inquisitive mind and strong work ethic.

If Seth were picking a new CEO, he'd definitely go for Gary Adams over Paul Bailey, despite the seeming disparity between the two men.

But he wasn't looking for a CEO.

He was looking for a killer. Which of the people on that list wanted the job badly enough to kill for it?

And why?

DELILAH HAMMOND HAD spent almost half her life away from Bitterwood and normally thought it a good thing. Her first eighteen years growing up on Smoky Ridge had been a long, exhausting exercise in avoidance. She'd dodged her father's blows and her mother's selfish neediness. She'd kept clear of Seth's self-destructive anger and the constant temptations of drugs, booze and sex, determined to get an education and get the hell out of the mountains with her future intact.

Good grades and hard work had earned her scholarships to college. More hard work had gotten her through the FBI Academy and onto a fast-paced domestic terrorism task force. Later, she'd left the bureau for the private sector and ended up where she was now, working for former marine Jesse Cooper and his family's security agency. She had a life. A purpose. Bitterwood, Tennessee, should have been in her rearview mirror, not her windshield.

But as she wound her way through the curves of Vesper Road toward Ivy Hawkins's house, closer and closer to the brushed-velvet peak of Smoky Ridge, she felt an odd, pulling sensation in the center of her chest.

Home, she thought, and bit her lip at the image. Just no getting away from it after all.

There was a black Jeep Wrangler parked in the driveway, she saw as she turned off Vesper Road. Ivy Hawkins was back.

As it turned out, so was Sutton Calhoun, Ivy's boyfriend and one of Delilah's oldest friends and a colleague at Cooper Security. He came out onto the porch before

Delilah had opened the driver's door of his truck, the expression on his tanned face fiercely grim.

Delilah's stomach cramped at the sight of him. Had something happened on his trip to northern Iraq? Nobody at Cooper Security had mentioned any trouble when she'd been there for the meeting last night.

"You're back," she greeted him, not bothering with a smile. He clearly wasn't in the mood.

Ivy Hawkins came out and stood beside him on the porch, her dark eyes blazing with anger. "Have you seen your brother lately?"

Oh, no, she thought. "Not since yesterday morning," she answered, climbing the steps slowly. "Why?"

Sutton gestured with his head for her to follow him inside the house. He led her into the study, where Ivy kept her computer. The laptop was open, and a photo of Rachel Davenport filled the screen.

Delilah walked closer, studying the photo with a frown. The photo had been taken at the funeral, she realized. Mourners were gathered around her, but she was definitely the focus of the image.

"Where did that come from?" She braced herself for the answer.

Sutton reached behind the laptop and pulled out a pair of sunglasses attached to a neck cord. It took a second look to realize the neck cord had a small connector jack built in. When Sutton picked up a small, rectangular plastic device and plugged in the cord, she realized what it really was.

"A spy camera." She looked up at Sutton. "Where'd you find this?"

"At my father's house." He put the unit down. "It was lying out in the open, next to the computer."

"And you think it's Seth's."

"Don't you?"

Delilah looked at the photo of Rachel Davenport still up on the computer screen. She'd caught Seth at the funeral and called him on being there, accusing him of trying to run some kind of con on Rachel.

He'd said he was there just to say goodbye to his employer. Clearly, he hadn't told her everything.

She closed her eyes. "How many photos?"

"About a hundred, spanning the past two weeks. He's been keeping an eye on Rachel Davenport primarily, although there were also some photos of the trucking company personnel. I don't know what your brother is up to, but it can't be good. He's put a hell of a lot of sweat and coin into following that woman around."

She forced herself to ask the obvious question, even though it made her sick to think about. "You think he's connected to the murders?"

The look of pity Sutton sent her way felt like a gut punch. "I honestly don't know."

"Where is Seth now?" Ivy asked. She was clipping her badge to the waistband of her jeans, Delilah realized.

"You're back on the job?" she asked. Ivy had been on administrative leave since Mark Bramlett's death.

"As of today," she said with a lopsided smile. "Never realized how much I'd want back on the job until I was forced off."

"What about you, Sutton? Still planning to give your notice and move back here to Hillbilly Heaven?"

Sutton put his hands on Ivy's shoulders. "Already gave my notice. The Iraq mission was my last one. I'm back in Bitterwood to stay."

Funny, Delilah thought, how a place so full of bad memories still had a way of getting under the skin. She'd never figured Sutton would come back to Bitterwood any more than she would. "Are you planning to arrest Seth?"

"Not sure we have what it takes to get a warrant," Ivy admitted. "But I'm definitely going to ask him a few questions."

"YOU SHOULD HAVE stayed with your uncle and aunt."

The first words Seth had spoken in almost two hours came out so soft she almost didn't hear them. She turned down the radio and met his brooding gaze. "I'm not going to hide in Bryson City. If someone's screwing around with my life, I have a right to know about it."

"That doesn't mean you have to be in the crosshairs."

"If this is your way of backing out of the investigation, just say so."

"I'm not saying that," he said quickly.

She turned onto the narrow, winding road that led to her family home, her stomach tensing as she thought about what might await her at the end of the road. She hadn't yet called the locksmith to change the locks nor gotten an estimate from an alarm company. Maybe she'd been depending on Seth Hammond too much. She needed to be able to meet Seth on equal footing, not as a victim. That's not the way she wanted him to think of her. Not by a long shot.

"If you want out, I'll understand. I don't want you to see me as an obligation.

His unnerving silence stretched out long enough for them to reach the end of her driveway. As she turned down the drive, his next words nearly ran her off onto the lawn. "I'm working for an FBI agent."

She righted the car, put on the brakes and looked at him. "What?"

"I've done some informant jobs for an FBI agent my

sister once worked with. Mostly undercover kind of stuff, places I could easily go that the FBI couldn't. A few weeks ago, just after Mark Bramlett died, my FBI handler called me and asked me to keep an eye on you."

Rachel pulled up outside the garage doors and parked, turning to look at Seth. He gazed back at her, clear-eyed.

"Why?" she asked.

"He didn't say exactly."

"You didn't ask?"

"I asked. He didn't say. All he told me is that this one wasn't for the FBI. It was personal."

"Personal?" That answer made even less sense than the FBI being interested in her life. "What's his name?"

Seth looked reluctant, but he finally answered, "Adam Brand. He's a special agent in charge in the Washington D.C. field office."

"I've never heard of him."

"I don't think it's that kind of personal."

"There's more than one kind of personal?"

He gave a soft huff of laughter. "There's all kinds of personal, sugar. But what I mean is, I got the feeling he's talking about your situation being of interest to him for a personal reason."

"And you didn't press him on it?"

"We've always had a need-to-know kind of relationship," he explained with a half smile. "If I need to know, he'll tell me. If he doesn't tell me, I don't need to know."

"You're okay with that?"

"I'm not crazy about it," he admitted. "But I've helped the FBI stop some very bad people from doing terrible things." His grimace suggested some of those terrible things had come very close to happening to him. "Adam Brand is one of the good guys, and there aren't many of them willing to give me a break."

"So what did Agent Brand ask you do to, where I'm concerned?"

"Just keep an eye on you."

"Is that why you were on the spot to help me at Purgatory Bridge?"

He shook his head. "That was dumb luck. I was just heading to Smoky Joe's for a good time."

"And ended up plucking my sorry backside off a bridge." She gave him an apologetic look.

"I'm glad I was there." The warmth in his voice seemed to spread to her bone marrow.

"So am I."

Silence fell between them, sizzling with unspoken desires. He wanted her—it burned in his eyes, scorching her—but he made no move to take what he wanted. What they both wanted.

She made no move, either, tethered in place by caution. Desire was a chemical thing that didn't always take reality into consideration. Wanting him wasn't a good enough reason to throw caution to the wind.

Was it?

"We need to get inside and see if anyone's left you any new surprises." He dragged his gaze away and opened the passenger door.

She stifled a sigh. Even if she was willing to take a chance, clearly Seth had different ideas.

Maybe it was for the best.

A thorough room-by-room inspection of the house showed no sign of an intruder. Seth took a second look around while Rachel was making calls to the locksmith and the alarm company that handled the trucking company's security. He wandered back downstairs as she was jotting down the appointment time she'd set with the security company for the following day.

"Did Delilah say when she'd be back from Alabama?" he asked, dropping onto the sofa across from where she sat.

"No. Why?"

"I need to go see Cleve at the hospital in Knoxville. I promised him I'd stop in at least once a week, and I'm running out of week."

"I think maybe you're running, period."

His gaze whipped up to meet hers. "Meaning?"

"Ignoring this thing between us doesn't make it go away."

His brow furrowed. "Rachel, we agreed—"

"What scares you about it?" she asked.

"It scares me that you're not scared," he answered flatly. "You're a smart woman. You've got to know that I'm a risky bet."

"Every relationship is a risk."

"You've lost a lot already. You're vulnerable and lonely—"

"So, I'm emotionally incapable of knowing what I want? Is that what you're suggesting?"

He closed his eyes a moment, frustration lining his sharp features. When he opened his eyes, they blazed with helpless need. "You're a beautiful woman. You seem so cool and composed on the outside, but then you give me this glimpse of the passion you got roiling around inside you and I just want to bathe myself in it." Raw desire edged his voice. "I've got no right to want you so damned much, but I do. And if you don't stop me, I don't know if I can stop myself."

She felt the last fragile thread of caution snap, plunging her into the scary, exhilarating ether of pure, blind faith. She rose from the sofa and walked over to where he sat.

"I don't want to stop you." She touched his face, sliding her fingers along the edge of his jaw. "Don't stop."

He turned his face toward her touch, his eyes drifting closed. "Rachel—"

Bending, she pressed her mouth to his, thrilling as his lips parted beneath hers, his tongue brushing over her lower lip and slipping between her teeth to tangle with her own tongue. He tasted like sweet tea and sin.

He wrapped his arms around her waist, pulling her down to him until her legs straddled his. She settled over his lap, acutely aware of the hard ridge of his erection against her own sex. A guttural sound rose in her chest as she pressed her body more firmly against his, molding herself around the hard muscles and flat planes of his body.

His hands slid down her back and curved over her bottom, his fingers digging into the flesh there, pulling her even closer. His breath exploded from his throat when she rocked against him, building delicious friction between their bodies.

"What am I going to do with you?" he groaned against her throat, his lips tracing a fiery path along the tendons of her neck.

She whispered her answer in his ear and eased off his lap, pushing to her feet. She held out her hand, locking gazes with him.

She saw questions there, but also a fierce, blazing desire to give her what she'd asked for. Slowly, his hand rose and clasped hers, and he let her tug him to his feet.

Their bodies collided, tangled, then melded. He wrapped one arm around her waist, pulling her against him, while his free hand threaded through her hair to tug her head back. He claimed her mouth in a slow, hot kiss, no frantic clash of teeth and tongues but a thorough seduction, full of purpose and promise.

"You look so prim and proper on the outside," he whispered against her temple as he led her to the stairs. "But you've got a danger monkey inside you."

She laughed at the term. "Danger monkey?"

He didn't answer until they'd reached the door of her bedroom. He stopped there, turning to look at her. As always, the intensity of his gaze made her legs wobble a little, and she grabbed the front of his shirt to hold herself upright.

"Being with me is a risk, Rachel. People will look at you differently. They'll tell you you're crazy. Tell me you know that."

She could barely catch her breath, but she managed to find the words. "I know that. I don't care." Growing impatient, she tugged the hem of his T-shirt upward, baring the flat plane of his belly to her wandering hands. She splayed her fingers over his stomach and ran them upward, through the crisp dark hairs of his torso. They tangled in the light thatch on his chest, drawing a low groan from his throat.

Then her fingers ran across the rough flesh of his burn scar, and he froze.

Her gaze lifted to meet his. "Is that where you were burned?"

He nodded. "One of the places."

"Let me see."

He slid his shirt off, baring the scars on his chest and shoulder. She examined them first with her gaze, then with a featherlight touch of her fingers. "It must have hurt like hell."

"It did. They told me at the hospital that I was lucky.

Most of my burns were second degree, which would heal better. But one of the doctors said they also hurt worse."

"Your mother must have considered you her hero."

Her words seemed to wound him. "My mother stayed drunk for days after the fire. All she ever said to me was that I should have saved my father, too. I didn't have the heart to tell her there wasn't enough left of him after the explosion to save."

Rachel pressed her cheek against his scarred shoulder. "I'm sorry. That must have been so terrible for you."

He threaded his fingers through her hair and made her look at him. "Don't feel sorry for me. That's one thing I don't need from you."

Her pity melted in a scorching blaze of desire. "Okay. So what's one thing you *do* need from me?"

He dipped his head and kissed her again. She heard the rattle of the doorknob as he groped for it, felt the shift of their bodies as he backed into the bedroom, drawing her along with him.

The backs of her knees connected with the bed, and she tumbled backward onto the mattress, Seth's body falling with her. He settled into the cradle of her thighs, dragging his mouth away from hers.

"I've never wanted anything as much as I want you," he whispered.

A thrill of power coursed through her, making her heart pound and her head spin. She rolled him over until she was on top of him, her hands clasped with his, pinning him to the mattress. She lowered her head slowly, kissing her way from his clavicle to the sharp edge of his jaw. She stopped, finally, at the curve of his ear, nipping lightly at the lobe.

"Prove it," she answered.

With catlike grace, he flipped her onto her back again, feral desire blazing from his eyes.

Slowly, thoroughly, he did as she'd asked.

Chapter Fourteen

"What did you want to be when you grew up?"

Rachel's sleepy voice pierced the hazy cloud of contentment on which Seth had been floating for the past few minutes. He roused himself enough to think about what she'd asked. "I think mostly I just wanted to grow up."

Her fingers walked lightly up his chest. "I guess there wasn't much room for dreams in that kind of life, huh?"

"I think the dreams were all unattainable on purpose," he answered after a moment of thought. "If you let yourself dream small, there was the possibility that it could come true. Which meant it hurt all the more when it didn't. But if you dreamed big, you knew from the start that it was impossible. So it couldn't really hurt you."

She was quiet for a long moment. "I used to want to be a writer."

"You did?" He supposed he could see it. She'd been a librarian, and her house was full of books. The temptation to create rather than simply consume was strong. He knew from his own experiences working as a mechanic the pleasure of being an active part of making something work. He'd always loved cars, even as a kid when having one of his own had seemed an impossibility. But he loved working on them even more, seeing what made them go, what could make them stop, how to make them work more efficiently.

"I did. But my father was always such a pragmatist. He liked to point out the odds against success in any endeavor. I don't think it occurred to me until much later on that he wasn't meaning to discourage me. He just wanted me to have the facts."

"And you let the facts deter you."

"I found an easier way to work with books."

"Easier isn't always better."

Rachel propped her head on her hand and looked down at him, her honey-brown hair falling in a curtain over his shoulder. "That's a very wise observation."

He laughed, shaking his head. "That's just bad experiences talking, sugar, not wisdom."

"Where you do think wisdom comes from?" She bent and kissed the scar on his chest, then touched it with her forefinger. "You checked the stove for a burner the other day."

He grimaced. "Fire and I don't mix well."

She slapped his chest lightly, making it sting in an oddly pleasurable way. "Like heights and me."

"You run from things that are bad for you." He gave her a pointed look. "Usually."

She rolled onto her back. "Stop it, Seth."

He turned onto his side to look at her, propping himself up on his elbow. She was only half-covered by the tangled sheets, her torso gloriously naked. In the golden late afternoon light slanting across the bed, she looked like a gilded goddess, all perfect curves and mysterious, shadowy clefts. She belonged in a better place than this, he thought. She deserved to be worshipped and adored by a worthy man.

What if he could never be that worthy, no matter how hard he tried?

"When I'm with you, I want to be perfect."

She met his gaze with smiling eyes. "Nobody's perfect."

"Wrong answer, gorgeous. You're supposed to say, 'But you are perfect, Seth. You're perfectly perfect. There's never been anyone more perfect in the history of the world.'"

She laughed. "Nobody sane would say that."

"Thanks a lot."

"I don't want perfect." She rose up on her elbow as well, facing him. "I want someone who makes the effort to do the right thing for the right reasons. When I look at you, when I watch you dealing with all the suspicion and temptations you have to deal with, that's what I see. I see a man who's made terrible mistakes that he still suffers for, but he tries. He tries so hard to be a better man."

Her words scared him. "What if I'm not that man?"

"You are," she insisted, pressing her hand flat on his chest. "You're just afraid to believe it."

He wanted to believe it. He had spent the first fifteen years of his life wishing away reality and he'd spent the last five years doing the same thing, though for different reasons.

Dreaming the impossible because it hurt less when it didn't come true.

But what if those dreams weren't really impossible? What if he could have a decent life, surrounded with good people who cared about him and wanted the best for him? Other people could live that life—what if he could, too? Was that really too impossible to believe?

A distant rapping sound filtered past his thoughts. After a few seconds of silence, the sound came again.

Rachel's head lifted toward the bedroom door. "Is that someone knocking on the door?"

The rapping downstairs had grown more insistent. With a low growl of impatience, Rachel swung her legs over the side of the bed and started gathering up her clothes, dressing as she went. Seth shrugged on his own clothes, joining her downstairs at the door.

"Wait." He put his arm in front of her as she started to open the door, holding her back. "Let me see who it is first."

He put one eye to the peephole and felt a ripple of surprise. Sutton Calhoun's face stared back at him through the fisheye lens.

"Who is it?" Rachel asked.

"An old friend." *Turned enemy,* he added silently. He unlocked the door and opened it.

The indistinct, distorted images that had flanked Sutton in the fisheye lens turned out to be Seth's sister, Delilah, and small, dark-eyed Detective Ivy Hawkins. Seth didn't know what he found more alarming, the grim looks on all three faces or the Bitterwood P.D. badge clipped to the front of Ivy's belt.

"Has something happened?" he asked.

"Seth Hammond, the Bitterwood Police Department would like to ask you some questions," Ivy said in a low, serious tone.

The sinking sensation in his chest intensified. "About what?"

Ivy's dark eyes flickered toward Rachel. "Your involvement in the harassment and stalking of Rachel Davenport."

"That's ridiculous," Rachel exclaimed, stepping forward. "Seth is not stalking me."

"We've found a disk of photos that would suggest otherwise," Sutton snapped, his gaze firmly fixed on Seth's face. Seth didn't miss the disgust, tinged with disappointment, in his old friend's eyes.

"You think I'm behind what's been happening to Rachel," he said.

"I saw the photos." Delilah sounded more hurt than angry. "I saw the sunglasses camera—that's expensive equipment. Where did you get the money?"

"Sunglasses camera?" For the first time, Rachel's voice held a hint of uncertainty.

"You were wearing them at the funeral," Delilah said, her gaze pleading with him to give her a reasonable excuse.

"He was snapping photos of you at your father's funeral," Sutton said.

Seth felt Rachel's gaze on him. He turned slowly to look at her.

Her blue eyes were dark with questions. "You were wearing sunglasses at the funeral. I remember that."

"I was," he agreed. "And they were camera glasses. Remember, I told you I was working for the FBI."

For a moment, some of the doubt cleared from Rachel's expression.

"Working for the FBI?" Delilah stared at him. "But how? You'd have had to pass background checks—" She stopped, shaking her head. "Seth, please—"

She wanted to believe him, he saw with some surprise. More than she doubted him. "Call Adam Brand," he said quietly. Urgently.

Delilah blanched at the mention of Brand's name, not for the first time. Seth had long suspected something bad had gone down between his sister and the FBI agent almost eight years earlier, when she was still working for the bureau.

Ivy pulled her phone from her pocket. "I'll call him."

As Delilah recited the D.C. office number from memory, Seth slanted a look at Rachel. She gazed back at him, trying to look supportive, but doubts circled in her blue eyes like crows in a winter sky.

"I'm not lying about this," he told her. But listening to his low, urgent tone, he could see why the doubt didn't immediately clear from her eyes. He sounded desperate and scared.

Because he was.

"He's not in his office," Ivy told them a moment later. "The person who answered said he'd taken a few days off and was out of pocket."

Seth frowned. Brand hadn't said anything to him about going on vacation. In fact, in all the time he'd been dealing with Brand, the man hadn't taken more than a day or two off at a time.

"He never goes on vacation," Delilah murmured, echoing his own thoughts.

"Why don't we go down to the station and sort through all of this?" Ivy suggested in a calm, commanding tone. Seth looked at her thoughtfully, remembering when she'd been a snot-nosed little brat who'd followed him and Sutton all over Smoky Ridge. She'd grown up, he realized, into a tough little bird.

He looked at Rachel again. Her eyes were on Delilah, her expression pensive. Seth followed her gaze and saw his sister staring at him with blazing hope rather than doubt.

She believed him, he realized with astonishment. "We'll keep calling," Delilah said quietly.

Sutton, however, was having none of it. "What's the point? You really think the FBI's going to hire a con man to keep tabs on a grieving heiress? That's like assigning an alligator to guard the pigpen."

Seth turned to look at Rachel. Her eyes had gone reflective. He couldn't tell what she was thinking, and that scared him to death. "Rachel—"

"Are you going to take him in?" She turned her cool gaze to Ivy.

Ivy nodded. "Yeah. I am."

Seth looked from Sutton's stony face to Ivy's. "You gonna cuff me?"

Ivy's left eyebrow peaked. "Is it going to be necessary?"

He was tempted to make it so. Go out in a blaze, since it's what everyone seemed to expect of him.

But he simply shook his head. "Let's get this over with."

He looked back as he walked out of the door, hoping to catch Rachel's eye and try one last time to make her see that he was telling the truth.

But she had turned away, her cell phone to her ear.

He trudged down the porch steps, feeling suddenly dead to the core.

RACHEL STOOD BENEATH the hot shower spray, her mind racing. She'd never been a woman of impulse, heedless of warning signs. Even as a child, she'd been a rule follower, thanks to her father, who'd always explained the reasons behind his strictures in ways she could understand.

Logic told her she should be down there at the police station right now, demanding that Seth explain his lies and machinations. But she just couldn't believe any of the allegations against him.

She knew all the reasons she should, of course. Though nobody had showed her any pictures, she didn't doubt they existed. Ivy Hawkins was a cop with no reason to lie. And even Seth's own sister had said she'd seen the photos.

But that didn't mean Seth had been doing something to hurt her. He'd told her he was working for the FBI, and she'd believed him. If he was following her on the orders of the mysterious Adam Brand, it made sense he might use covert surveillance equipment to do so.

She'd called the trucking company as soon as Ivy Hawkins had made it clear she was taking Seth in for questioning, wondering if there was any sort of fund available from the company to help employees with legal problems. But their lawyer had been doubtful. "What you're describing doesn't sound as if it's connected to the employee's work at the company," Alice Barton had told her. "He wouldn't qualify."

She'd known the legal fund idea was a long shot, but she had a feeling Seth might have been more open to accepting her help if it came from the company instead of her own resources. No matter. She was going to figure out a way to help him whether he liked it or not.

Out of the shower, she dressed quickly, letting her hair air dry as she pondered what to do next. She needed to see the photos, she realized. See the so-called evidence against Seth. There might be something in those photos that could clue her in to who was really trying to destroy her life.

Before Delilah had dropped her off at her car the day after the Purgatory Bridge incident, she'd given Rachel her business card with her cell phone number. Where had she put it?

She was digging through the drawers of her writing desk, looking for the card, when there was another insistent knock on the door. Distracted, she almost opened the door without looking through the peephole. She stopped at the last moment and took a peek.

It was her stepbrother, Paul.

Relaxing, she opened the door. "Oh. Hi."

He pushed past her into the house. He looked around, as if he expected to find someone else there with her. "Are you okay?"

"What's wrong?" she asked, closing the door behind them.

"I just got a call from Jim Hallifax at the locksmith's place down the street from the office. He said you were changing the locks here because you'd had an incident with an intruder."

She stared at him, confused. "Why on earth would Jim Hallifax call you about that?"

Paul stared back at her a moment, looking a little sheepish. "I, uh, mentioned in passing that you were taking your father's death badly and that I was worried about you being here all alone. I guess he thought I'd want to know that you'd had some trouble."

She shook her head. "He had no business telling you that."

"Are you angry that I know?"

She took a deep breath and let it out slowly. "No. But I'm fine. Really." At least, she had been while Seth was there. Now that she was alone, however, she felt vulnerable again.

"You shouldn't stay here alone. I could move in for a little while, at least until the locks are changed."

"I'm getting an alarm put in, too," she assured him. "Dad resisted it forever, but I just don't think it's safe to live here without some form of protection."

The phone rang, interrupting whatever Paul was going to say in response. For a second, Rachel thought it might be Seth, but she realized he'd have called her cell phone. She let it ring, not in the mood to talk to anyone else at the moment. The machine would pick up the message.

"Call from Brantley's Garage," the mechanized voice drifted in from the hallway where the phone was located. Rachel frowned, trying to remember why Brantley's Garage would be calling. As the message beep sounded, she remembered. Seth's car with the flat tires. They'd given Brantley her phone number in case he couldn't be reached by his cell.

She didn't reach the phone before the caller started leaving a message. "Mr. Hammond, this is Wally from Brantley's Garage. Your car is ready to pick up."

She grabbed the phone. "Wally, Mr. Hammond isn't here, but I'll be sure he gets the message. Thanks." Bracing herself, she hung up the phone and turned to look at her stepbrother.

He stared at her, his expression disbelieving. "Why would the garage call here to reach Seth Hammond?"

"Because he was staying here with me."

Paul stared at her as if she'd lost her mind. "Why?"

She sighed, realizing she was going to have to tell someone everything that had happened, sooner or later. There was no point in trying to hide from her choices any longer. She'd made them, and if they turned out to be mistakes, she'd have to live with them, because she had no intention of apologizing.

"It's a long story," she said. "And it started a couple of nights ago on Purgatory Bridge."

Chapter Fifteen

"Are you charging me with something?" Seth blurted before Ivy Hawkins and Antoine Parsons asked the first question.

"Should we?" Ivy asked.

"Charge me or let me go," he said flatly.

"We can hold you for twenty-four hours without charging you for anything," Antoine said in a quiet tone. "I'd rather not do either, frankly. I'd like to believe you've gotten your act together, because I remember you as being an okay guy back in the day, before all that mess went down with your dad and you got sucked into Cleve Calhoun's world."

So, Seth thought, *Parsons gets to be the good cop.* He looked at Ivy, who was watching him with thoughtful eyes. "I've told you everything. Meanwhile, Rachel Davenport is home alone at a house that's been broken into at least once, after over a month of incidents targeting her and the people around her. Including five murders."

"Why did the FBI want you to keep an eye on Rachel Davenport?" Antoine asked.

"Adam Brand didn't say. All he told me was that it wasn't an official FBI inquiry."

"Was that unusual?"

"Never happened before," he admitted.

"And you didn't question the order?" Ivy interjected.

"Of course I did. But look—Adam Brand's an FBI agent, which means he's a secretive guy by default. He tells me only what he thinks I need to know in order to do the job he gives me. I didn't need to know why I was keeping an eye on Rachel."

"You weren't even curious?" Ivy sounded doubtful.

"Honestly? I didn't care. I was already keeping an eye on Rachel before he called." He gave her a pointed look. "But you already know that."

He saw Antoine slant a quick look at Ivy and realized the pretty little police detective apparently hadn't done much talking with her partner about Seth's part in bringing down serial killer Mark Bramlett. He supposed she might not have had time to tell him much before the police department put her on administrative leave.

"I certainly didn't know you were stalking her," Ivy denied.

"I'm not stalking her," he protested, though he supposed that an outside observer might think so. He'd been spending many of his off-work hours keeping an eye on Rachel Davenport and the people around her, ever since he'd started putting two and two together about the serial killer victims, all of whom had shared a connection with Rachel.

"You've been following her. Taking photos of her. Insinuating yourself in her life. Know what that sounds like to me?" she asked.

"Like a con man picking out a new mark," he answered.

She looked a little surprised to hear him say it out loud. "Then you see the issue I have with your story."

"And here's the issue I have with the way your department has handled this investigation," he snapped back.

"It took four murders before you'd so much as admit in public you were looking for a serial killer. And it took you longer still to tie all four people to Rachel Davenport."

"You knew earlier?" Antoine asked with a slight rise of one dark brow.

"Y'all never step foot into any of the beer joints around these parts, do you?" He shook his head. "You like to sit here in your nice, clean police station and pretend there's not any crime in these parts, not like there is in the big city, even though these hills are full of desperate, poor people. That's why someone can offer twenty grand to kill someone and you'll never hear a word of it, because you're too scared to get down in the dirt where the bad guys wallow."

Antoine looked surprised. But not Ivy. Because she was sleeping with Sutton Calhoun, of course. They were talking marriage and babies and the whole sappy lot, from what Seth had heard. Of course, Sutton had told her what Seth had told him about the twenty-grand hit he'd heard about.

"Sutton told me about that," Ivy said quietly. She gave Antoine an apologetic look. "I should have told you. I'm sorry. It was only hearsay, and Sutton didn't know who Seth had talked to."

"It would have helped with our investigation," he said. "You want to tell us who told you?"

"The guy's nowhere around these parts anymore. He got out of town not long after that happened. I don't even know his real name. Just the name he went by when we crossed paths now and then. Calls himself Luke, but he's fast to tell you it's short for Lucifer, because he's a fallen angel." Seth grimaced. "My theory, he's some poor preacher's black sheep son. His mama probably prays for him every night and cries about him every day."

"What did Luke tell you, exactly?" Antoine asked.

"That he had been offered a hit job."

"And you didn't think to mention this to us before now?"

"Luke didn't take the job, and if you snatched him up, he'd know I was the one who told. I might need information from him in the future."

Ivy's brow furrowed. "Information for what?"

"Anything. Everything." Seth leaned forward. "You don't know what it's like living outside proper society, do you? Sure, your mama's got a bit of a reputation for bringing home deadbeats, but people mostly understood that was just because she wanted someone to love her. They may not have approved, and I'm sure some of them thought she was stupid, but nobody ever thought she was a bad person."

Ivy gave a slight nod.

"Right now, I can't depend on society to see me as anything but trouble. And I'm not lookin' for sympathy when I say that—I know I brought on my own troubles. But it doesn't change my situation. There are times when I have to depend on people you wouldn't want to be seen with. Hell, I don't want to be seen with 'em, not anymore, because it makes it that much harder for me to try to fit in with good people." He shook his head. "But my opinion of what constitutes good people and bad people can be a little fluid."

He saw a hint of sympathy in Ivy's dark eyes. "Did you press Luke about who tried to hire him?"

"Not at the time. I hadn't connected it to the Davenports then. I was trying to keep my nose clean, stay out of messes, and I didn't want to know anything more." He felt a sharp pang of guilt. "If I'd pushed a little harder, maybe I could have stopped it. But I just wanted to stay clear of trouble."

"You should have told us," Antoine agreed. "Do you have any idea how to find this Luke person again?"

"I tried to find him a few weeks ago, but he wasn't anywhere around. I talked to some mutual acquaintances and they told me Luke had gone to Atlanta for a while to see if he could get any work down there."

"What kind of work did he do?"

Seth shot Antoine a pointed look.

"The kind of work you used to do?"

"Yeah, he runs cons when he can. If you can get your hands on Atlanta area mug shots from bunco arrests in the past three weeks, I could maybe pick him out of a lineup."

"We'll look into that," Ivy said. "Meanwhile, there's the issue of the photos you took of the funeral."

"I told you what that was about."

"And conveniently, your so-called contact at the FBI is out of pocket."

"Not very damned convenient for me," Seth disagreed. "And how many times do we have to go back over this same ground? You do realize you've left Rachel Davenport by herself, unprotected, in order to chase me around in circles for no good reason?"

Ivy and Antoine exchanged looks. As if they'd reached a silent agreement, Antoine got up and exited the interview room, leaving Ivy alone with Seth.

"Where's he going?"

"He'll get someone to check on Ms. Davenport."

"Look, Ivy—Detective." He couldn't help but make a little face as he corrected himself, a picture in his mind of Ivy Hawkins as a snub-nosed thirteen-year-old with shaggy hair, skinned knees and a crooked grin. It was hard to take her seriously as a police officer when he'd known her as a tagalong for so many years. "I know why you have to bring me in and ask me these questions. I'm trying to be patient and cooperative. I am. But you and Sutton painted a really bad picture of me for Rachel. I've been trying to help her, not hurt her. And it's got to be hard for her to trust anyone, especially someone like me—"

Ivy's eyes widened. "Oh my God. Are you involved with her?"

He sat back in consternation.

"Oh my God." Ivy sat back, too, staring across the table at him through widened eyes. "What exactly did we interrupt this afternoon?"

He made himself as opaque as he could and didn't answer.

"Oh my God."

"Will you please stop saying that?" he asked.

Ivy brought her hand up to her mouth, covering it as if it were the only way to keep from blurting out her shock again. The resulting image would have been comical if Seth hadn't been so worried.

A knock on the door drew Ivy out of her seat. A uniformed officer told her something, and she turned to Seth. "Stay here. I'll be right back."

"Is something up?"

"I'll be back in a minute." Ivy left the interview room, closing the door behind her.

Seth put his head in his hands, frustrated by the delay. Rachel probably thought the worst of him right now. And who could blame her? He'd kept things secret, as usual, not trusting her with the full measure of truth. He talked a good game about trying to earn her trust, but when it came right down to it, he hadn't trusted her enough to be completely honest.

And now, he had to pay for it. He just prayed Rachel didn't have to pay for it, as well. Because she'd already been alone in that house for too long, without anyone to protect her from whoever wanted to do her harm.

"You should have told me about all of this." Paul gave Rachel a stern look softened slightly by the sympathy in his brown eyes. "Why did you try to go through all of this alone?"

"I wasn't alone."

"And trusting a man like Seth Hammond is even crazier."

"He was very kind to me. He's taken some risks to help me out," she defended Seth, wondering why she was bothering. Paul would look at the evidence and assume the worst. Seth had tried to warn her that's how it would be. To anyone on the outside, all the evidence would seem to point to Seth's playing games with her. If she hadn't spent the past few days getting to know Seth intimately, she might concur.

Intellectually, she could see the warning signs, but she couldn't connect them to the Seth Hammond she knew. He had been nothing but kind to her, even when telling her a few hard truths. He'd been genuinely remorseful about the ways he'd hurt people in the past. He'd told her the truth when a lie would have served him better.

"Why would someone do all of this to you?" Paul asked her.

"I think it must have something to do with Davenport Trucking. Or, more specifically, my job there."

Paul's brow furrowed. "In what possible way?"

"Paul, what do you know about my father's will?"

He shrugged. "Only what scuttlebutt at the office says. Your father wanted you to be CEO when he died, and so you will be."

"Have you ever heard anyone speculating about what might happen if I weren't able to take the job?"

"Not that, exactly." Paul pressed his mouth into a thin line. "I guess people are wondering why you'd want the job. You always loved being a librarian. I think some people thought George was being unfair to ask you to take over his dream by leaving your own dream behind."

She'd felt the same way, at first. And felt a hell of a lot of guilt about it, considering her father's deteriorating condition. "I need them to realize I'm doing this job because I want to, not because I feel obligated to."

"Is that really how you feel?" Paul looked unconvinced.

"At least for the next few years."

"And then?"

"And then we'll see." She had a feeling she'd go back to the library sooner or later. But not before she was certain her father's legacy was in the best hands possible. She owed her father's memory that much.

He was silent for a long moment. "It would be easier on you if you stepped down."

"I'm not going to let someone scare me away from a job I've decided to do." She lifted her chin.

"You really think these murders are about you?"

"I know it sounds crazy."

"It sounds narcissistic," he said.

"It's neither. It's just what the evidence is pointing to. You think I want to believe people have been murdered to get to me? Believe me, I don't."

"But you've been listening to Seth Hammond. He's

not exactly the most reliable of tale-tellers. What if he's playing his own game with you?"

"I've thought about that." She'd thought about it a lot, especially over the past hour, testing her faith in him against the logic her father had taught her. "I just don't see what he gets out of it."

"Do you know how he used to make a living?"

"He was a con man."

"He was a particular kind of con man. He preyed on vulnerable women. Convinced them that he wanted them, that he loved them. That they should trust him. He bilked them, and then he was gone."

She didn't answer, knowing he wasn't telling her anything that Seth would deny.

"You're not falling for him, are you?"

"I know what he is," she answered. Her cell phone rang. She dug it from her pocket and saw an unfamiliar local number.

Was it Seth? He might be stuck at the police station, using his one phone call to get in touch with her. She punched the button and answered the call.

It wasn't Seth. It was a police officer. "Ms. Davenport, this is Jerry Polito with the Bitterwood Police Department. Detective Antoine Parsons asked me to check on you, see if you're okay there by yourself."

"I'm not by myself, Officer," she answered with a look at Paul. "My stepbrother is here."

"Good." The policeman sounded relieved. "Detective Parsons suggested you might want to have someone stay with you, given all that's been happening to you."

"Thank you." She hung up and turned to Paul. "The police. They were concerned about having left me here alone."

"You're not alone." Paul put his hand on her shoulder. "I'll stick around tonight, okay?"

He had stayed there plenty of times during his mother's marriage to her father, but she couldn't shake the feeling that she'd prefer to be alone than to have Paul stick around for the night. Maybe it was as simple as wanting to be free from scrutiny or unwelcome pity for a while.

And, if she was being honest with herself, she was hoping Seth would be released soon and come back to finish what they'd started that morning.

God, she needed to talk to him. She needed to hear his voice, to make sure he was okay.

"Why don't I make you some tea?" Paul suggested, nudging her toward the kitchen. "You still have some of that honey chamomile stuff you and my mom like so much?"

"I think so." She followed him into the warm room at the back of the house, trying not to remember the time she'd spent in there with Seth just that morning.

But the kitchen was no worse than the den, where she'd begun her earnest seduction of the most dangerous man she knew. Or the hallway, where they'd kissed up against the wall for a long, breathless moment before finding their way to the bedroom.

Even after her shower, she'd imagined she could still smell him on herself, a rich, musky male scent that made her toes curl and her heart pound. She wanted him there with her. Where he belonged. If he walked through the front door that very minute, she knew she'd tell Paul to go home and leave her alone with Seth. To hell with what Paul thought about it.

To hell with what anyone thought.

"PAUL BAILEY HAS a record," Ivy told Antoine. She spoke too quietly for Seth to hear her from his seat at the interview table, but he'd long ago learned how to read lips. Cleve had pounded into him the importance of equipping himself with all the tools necessary to do a thorough con job.

Being able to tell what people were discussing while out of earshot was just one of his skills. Another was reading body language. And Ivy Hawkins's body language screamed anxiety.

Antoine Parsons looked at the folder Ivy showed him, his brow furrowed. The anxiety seeped from her body into his, setting up a low, uneasy vibration in the room.

Seth couldn't stand the wait. "Why did you look at Paul Bailey's record?"

Both of the detectives turned to look at him as if they'd forgotten he was still in the room. "We've been looking at everyone at Davenport Trucking." Antoine sounded distracted. "The records from Mississippi just came through. He had some gambling problems when he was working casinos there. It's how he lost his job—skimming and setting up some cheats for money."

Seth sat back in his chair, surprised. He'd never thought of Paul Bailey as a possible suspect. The guy didn't seem interesting enough to earn suspicion.

"Even if he has a gambling problem, I'm not sure how taking control of Davenport Trucking could help him," Ivy answered. "I did some looking into the company back during the murder investigation. The CEO position's compensation package isn't all that large. Most of the profits are funneled back into the company. If Paul were to be made CEO, at most his pay would go up a hundred thousand."

"That's a lot of money," Antoine murmured.

"It can't just be about money," Seth said. "If he's the guy behind it, he was out there offering twenty grand for the hit. If he's so money-strapped, how can he pay twenty grand?"

Ivy and Antoine exchanged looks. "If it's not about money, what's it about?"

"I never said it wasn't about money. I said it's not *just* about money." Seth stood up from the interview table, bracing himself for one or both of the detectives to tell him to sit back down. But they didn't, so he continued, "I've been trying to figure out why anyone would target Rachel Davenport in the particular way they have, and it's got to be about Davenport Trucking, right? All the evidence points in that direction."

Ivy nodded slowly. "Agreed."

"Whoever targeted Rachel didn't kill her, because killing her creates a different set of events than just getting her out of contention for the job."

"What different set of events?" Antoine asked.

Seth outlined what he'd learned about the triggers that came into play depending on how the CEO job came to be vacated. "If she's dead, control of the company goes to her uncle Rafe, and he makes all the decisions without input from the trustees. But if she's merely incapacitated, the trustees make a decision based on recommendations already in place. There's a list of preapproved candidates for CEO. Paul Bailey, by the way, is one of those preapproved candidates."

"Does he know he's one of the candidates?"

"Probably. His mama is one of the trustees, and they seem to have a close relationship. Plus, from what Rachel's told me, Paul hasn't always been gung ho about working for the company, so I figure there must have been discussions between George Davenport and Paul for the old man to feel okay about including him on that list of candidates."

"But if the compensation's not that much better——" Antoine began.

"That's what's been bugging the hell out of me," Seth admitted. "But while I was waiting for y'all to get back in here, I started thinking about what the job would entail besides just money. It's long hours and a lot of stress, because you've got dozens of trucks at your command and you're responsible for where they go, what they haul, what fines have to be paid if you screw things up, what repairs and regular maintenance have to be done, and suddenly it hit me that I needed to stop thinking about it as a businessman and start considering how I might use it if I had criminal intentions."

Ivy shot him an amused look. "What a stretch for you."

He made a face at her. "If I was criminally inclined these days, there's a hell of a lot I could do with a fleet of trucks. I could move drugs back and forth. Illegal arms. Hell, I could traffic in people. Sex slaves, illegals, anything and everything. I could haul a dirty bomb from Central America to Washington, D.C., if I had my own fleet of trucks."

"I'm glad you don't," Antoine murmured.

"My point is, control of the trucks is control of a lot of potential income. If someone was inclined to use even a tenth of the fleet for illicit purposes——"

"They could make a fortune," Ivy finished for him.

There was a knock on the interview room door. Antoine grimaced at the interruption and went to answer the knock.

"If Paul Bailey still has a gambling problem, maybe he owes somebody very bad a lot of money," Ivy said grimly.

"It could be the mob, the Redneck Mafia, South American money launderers—"

"Could be anyone who wants to control a fleet of trucks for the small price of forgiving Paul Bailey's gambling debt," Ivy said. "Good God."

"And he's there with Rachel right now," Antoine said from the doorway, his expression dark. A uniformed policeman stood behind him.

Seth snapped his gaze up. "What?"

"Jerry just talked to her on the phone. Her stepbrother is there with her. She said he was going to stay there so she wouldn't be alone."

"Damn it!" Seth started toward the door, ready to bowl them both over if they tried to stop him.

Neither of them did.

Chapter Sixteen

The chamomile tea was a little sweet for her taste, but Rachel wasn't going to complain. After the day she'd just survived, she wasn't about to be picky when someone gave her a little uncomplicated pampering.

Paul settled into the chair across from her at the kitchen table and sipped his own cup of tea. "I closed off that trapdoor to the attic while the tea was brewing."

"Yes, I know. I heard the hammering." She smiled.

"Speaking of the attic, I was actually planning to come here today before I talked to Jim Hallifax. Feel up to a little scavenger hunt?"

She raised her eyebrows over her cup of tea. "Scavenger hunt?"

"Mother called from Wilmington. She meant to take her wedding album with her to her sister's place but left it behind. I was planning to carry it with me when I visit her later this week, but I have no idea where she kept the album. She said she thought it might be in the attic?"

Rachel grimaced at the thought of going up there again. "I'm sure it's probably in an obvious place."

Paul gave her a teasing smile. "Oh, right, you're scared of high places, aren't you? Still haven't outgrown that?"

"It's not that, exactly." She stopped short of telling him what her phobia was really about. Funny, she thought, how she'd been able to share that deep, dark secret with Seth but balked at telling a man who was practically family. "And you're right. I should have outgrown it by now. Did Diane give you any idea where in the attic it might be?"

Paul smiled helplessly. "She said something about a box on the top of a bookshelf?"

Oh great, Rachel thought. *A high place within a high place.*

But this was a good test for her to prove, to herself if no one else, that she wasn't going to let her past define her any longer.

She put down her cup and pushed to her feet. "Fine. But you're coming with me to hold the stepladder."

"I KNEW YOU weren't involved with this." Delilah told Seth as they sped along the twists and turns of Copperhead Road, part of a three-vehicle rescue mission. Ivy's Jeep was in the lead, with Antoine right behind her. Delilah and Seth took up the rear, to his dismay, forced to go only as fast as the vehicles ahead of them.

"You knew?" He shot her a skeptical look.

"Okay, I wanted to believe." She looked apologetic.

"I'm in this to help Rachel."

"I know. I'm sorry I didn't see it sooner."

"There was a lot you had to look past first." He tamped down a potent mixture of frustration and fear as he tried Rachel's cell phone again. It went directly to voice mail. "Why the hell isn't she answering?"

"Did you try the home phone?"

"Yeah. I get a busy signal."

Delilah didn't respond, but he could tell from the grim set of her jaw that she was worried.

"I think I love her," he said, even though he'd meant to say something entirely different.

Delilah's gaze flicked toward him. "What?"

"I think I love Rachel." He shook his head and corrected himself. "I know I love her."

"Oh my God."

"Why do people keep saying that? You think I'm not capable of loving someone?"

"I didn't say that. It's just—surprising."

He slammed his hand against the dashboard. "Can't we go faster?"

"These mountain roads are treacherous at normal speeds," Delilah said. "At high speeds, we could all end up dead, and how's that going to help Rachel?"

His heart felt as if it were going to pound right out of his chest. "I shouldn't have let y'all leave there without her. I should've protected her better. Damn it!"

"When did this happen? This thing with Rachel?"

He stared at her. "We're going to talk about my love life in the middle of all this?"

"You brought it up."

"I don't know," he growled. "I always thought she was pretty, of course. And I guess when I started suspecting the murders had something to do with Davenport Trucking, I started paying more attention to her."

"You suspected a connection all along?"

"After the second murder, when it was clear that both of the dead women had worked at Davenport, yeah. I did."

"This is so crazy. Her stepbrother."

"If he's in debt to the mob or someone connected like that, his life is on the line. He's already proved he's willing to kill to stay alive. He's not going to stop just because his stepsister is next on the list." He tried to keep his voice calm, but inside he was raging.

If, God forbid, they arrived too late—

"Oh, no," Delilah murmured.

He looked at her and found her gazing through the windshield ahead, her brow furrowed. He followed her gaze and saw what she had.

Smoke, rising in a black column over the treetops.

Something straight ahead was on fire.

And the only thing straight ahead was Rachel's house.

THE SLAMMING OF the attic door had caught Rachel by surprise. Already nervous, she'd jumped and whirled at the sound, ready to scold Paul for scaring the wits out of her.

But Paul wasn't there.

"Paul?" She'd been certain he was right behind her on the ladder. She'd felt his footfalls on the rungs below her, making her cling all the more tightly to the ladder as she climbed.

He hadn't answered, but she'd heard noise on the other side of the door. Reaching down to push the attic door open again, she'd discovered it wouldn't budge. "Paul, damn it! This isn't funny!"

More sounds of movement had come from below, but Paul hadn't answered.

Then she'd smelled it. The pungent odor of gasoline. "Paul?"

She'd heard a faint hiss, then a louder crackling noise on the other side of the door. The smell of smoke mixing with the fuel odor had spurred her into full-blown panic mode.

She'd grabbed the metal hasp of the attic door again to give it a tug and found it hot as blazes, making her snatch her hand back with a hiss of pain.

Fire. The house is on fire.

She wasn't sure how long she'd stood frozen in place

after that, trying to think. Long enough to realize there was more than just panic going on. Her brain seemed oddly sluggish, as if it took thoughts a longer time than usual to make it from idea to action.

Had she been drugged? Had he given her something in the chamomile tea? Something to slow her reaction time, to muddy her thinking so that she couldn't escape his trap?

She needed help. She needed—

She needed her phone. Digging in the pocket of her jeans, she'd expelled a soft sigh of sheer relief at finding it there. But when she tried to make a call, there was no signal.

That's crazy, she'd thought, trying to quell her rising fear long enough to think past the cottony confusion swirling in her brain. The house was one of the few places in Bitterwood where there was almost never any trouble getting a signal.

Unless, she realized, someone had a jammer.

Paul. Oh, no. It couldn't be.

Okay, okay. Think. She obviously couldn't get out the way she'd come in. Smoke already poured into the attic through the narrow seams in the door. Even if Paul hadn't wedged it shut behind her somehow, the fire would make getting out that way impossible.

But there was another trap door by the window.

She was halfway there before she remembered that Paul had already nailed it shut. Stumbling over the last few steps, she came to a stop against the window frame, sagging in despair.

He'd planned this, she realized. He'd come here today not to protect her but to kill her.

But why? Did he want to run Davenport Trucking so badly that he'd kill her for it? How did that make any sense? He'd never seen the job as anything more than a paycheck. He didn't even go to Christmas parties or participate in any of the interoffice morale projects.

But his interest had picked up in the past few months, hadn't it?

Why?

She felt certain the answer was somewhere just beyond the mists in her brain, so close she could almost feel it.

She banged her hand against the wall in frustration. "Paul!" she shouted, wondering if he could hear her over the rising din of crackling flames. "Paul, if you want the CEO job, I'll give it to you. Right now. In writing. Paul!"

Hell, he was probably nowhere near the house by now. The police knew he'd been there as recently as thirty minutes ago. He was probably already gone, off to set up an alibi for himself.

She turned and looked out the window, staring down the dizzying twenty-five-foot drop to the flagstone patio below.

Paul was gone, and she was trapped in her worst nightmare.

A DARK SEDAN swept past them on Copperhead Road, traveling in the opposite direction. So intent was Seth on the expanding column of smoking rising ahead of them that he almost ignored the passing motorist.

But a faint flicker of recognition sparked in his brain as the sedan reached them and passed. "That's Paul Bailey's car!"

Delilah's head twisted as the other vehicle passed. She shoved her cell phone at Seth. "Hit the *S* button. Sutton's on my speed dial."

Sutton answered on the first ring. "What?"

"The dark blue Toyota Camry that just passed us going south—that's Paul Bailey's car. Go after him."

A moment later, Ivy's Jeep pulled a sharp U-turn and headed off after the sedan. Antoine's department sedan braked and turned, as well. He slowed as they started to pass, and Delilah put on the brakes, rolling down the window at his gesture.

"I've called in Fire and Rescue, but they're across town. It may be up to y'all to get her out." He gunned the engine and swept off in pursuit of Ivy's Jeep and Bailey's Toyota.

Delilah pressed the accelerator to the floor, forcing Seth to grab the dashboard and hang on.

The house almost looked normal at first glance, but smoke was pouring from somewhere on the second floor, rising over the slanted eaves to coil like a slithering snake in the darkening sky. Seth jumped out of the truck before it stopped rolling, racing for the front door at a clip.

Delilah's footsteps pounded behind him on the flagstone walkway. "You don't have any protective gear!"

He ignored her, not letting himself think about what lay on the other side of the door. Tried not to smell the smoke or hear the crackle of the fire's hissing taunts. The heat was greater the closer he got, but he pretended he didn't feel it, because if he let himself feel it, if he let himself picture the licking flames and skin-searing heat, he wasn't sure he could do what he had to do.

"Rachel!" he shouted, taking the porch steps two at a time. He reached for the door handle.

"No!" Delilah's small, compact body slammed into him, knocking him to the floor of the porch. He struggled with her, but she was stronger than he remembered, pinning him against the rough plank floor. "Stop. There could be a back draft if you open the door right now! We have to do this right."

He stared at her, his heart hammering against his sternum, each thud laced with growing despair. "What if she's already dead?"

Delilah's gaze softened. "We'll find a way in. I promise."

She let him up, holding out her hand to help him to his feet. He gingerly put his hand on the doorknob and found it sizzling hot to the touch. Fear gripped him, a cold, tight fist squeezing his intestines until he felt light-headed. He could see the flicker of flames already climbing the curtains of the front windows and tried not to collapse into complete panic.

"Maybe the fire hasn't reached the back," Delilah said, her hand closing around his arm.

The back. Of course. If the fire hadn't gotten to the back of the house—

He forced his trembling legs into action, speeding back down the porch steps and around the corner of the house.

The back of the house showed no sign of fire yet. Even if the rest of the house was in flames, if Rachel was holed up somewhere the fire hadn't reached, he might be able to get her out through the trapdoors in the mudroom and closet.

But to do that, he had to go inside.

Where the fire was.

"Seth!" Delilah caught up with him and grabbed his arm, pointing up.

He followed her gaze and saw a pale face gazing down at him through the open attic window. Smoke slithered out around her, coiling her in its sinister grasp.

"Rachel," he breathed. She was alive.

"The trapdoor's nailed...shut..." She swayed forward,

grabbing the window frame in time to keep from toppling out. "I think…I'm drugged."

"We need a ladder," Delilah said urgently. "A tall one."

"Rachel, do you have a ladder? A long one?"

"No ladders!" She shook her head, sagging against the window frame. "No ladders. Please, no ladders." The last came out weakly, and she disappeared from the window.

"She's terrified of heights," he told Delilah. "But that may be the only way to get her. Go check the shed over there for a ladder."

"What are you going to do?" she asked, her dark eyes wide.

"I'm going to see if I can undo whatever Paul did to the trapdoors and get her out that way." It would still involve ladders, but shorter ones, not a rickety steel nightmare.

He could spare her that much, couldn't he? Even if it meant facing his own worst nightmare?

"You're really going into the fire?" Delilah stared at him as if she were seeing him for the first time.

"I have to," he answered, and put his hand on the back doorknob. It was only mildly warm to the touch. Taking care, he opened the door. Heat billowed out to greet him, but it didn't trigger any sort of combustion. He looked at his sister. "Go find a ladder, in case I fail."

She gave him a final, considering look before jogging off to the shed.

He entered the mudroom and tried the trapdoor, surprised but relieved to find it unlocked. He climbed into the second-floor bedroom closet, coughing as smoke seeped in under the bedroom door and burned his lungs.

It was a lot hotter in the closet, but he didn't let himself think about it. He turned on the closet light, which made the thick cloud of smoke in the small room all the more visible. Covering his mouth with his sleeve, he reached for the ladder to the attic trapdoor and stopped, gazing up in dismay. The door wasn't just nailed closed. It had been anchored in place with at least two dozen long nails. Even if he had a hammer—which he didn't—it would take long, precious minutes to pull out all those nails. And the police had confiscated his Swiss Army knife.

Painfully aware of the ticking clock, he reversed course and went back through the mudroom door. The heat here was stronger, pouring around him in slick, greasy waves. The odor of gasoline wafted toward him, and he realized there was an open container sitting right by the back door.

He set it outside quickly and looked toward the shed. The door was open and Delilah was inside, digging around. "I need a hammer!" he called to her. "Can you see a hammer?"

She emerged from the shed a moment later, carrying a large, old-looking claw-head hammer. He met her halfway to get it.

"The fire is spreading," he told her breathlessly as he took the hammer. "Even if I get up to her, we may not have any choice but to get down by ladder. The sooner the better. I'm not sure we can wait for the fire trucks to arrive. Have you found a ladder?"

"I spotted it in the back. I have to dig for it. You get into the attic. I'll get the ladder." She squeezed his arm, encouragement shining in her dark eyes. Warmth spread through his whole body like a booster shot of hope.

"See you on the other side of the window," he said.

He raced back into the burning house, dismayed to discover that in the few brief seconds he'd been outside, fire had licked closer to the mudroom. He could see flames dancing through the kitchen doorway, spreading inexorably closer. By the time he made it into the attic, the mudroom exit wasn't likely to be a viable escape route.

It was going to be the ladder or nothing.

The heat in the bedroom closet was oppressive, though the door had not yet become engulfed in flames. Still, eerie yellow light flickered through the narrow slit beneath the door, and smoke pouring through the crack limited visibility in the crowded space to inches.

He pulled down the trapdoor ladder as far as it would go with the door nailed shut and hauled himself up on the rungs, praying the wood was sturdy enough to hold his weight while he worked. So far, the electricity in the house was still on, giving him enough light to see the nails he had to remove.

"Rachel?" he called, wondering if she could hear him on the other side of the trapdoor. Was she even conscious anymore?

"Seth?" Her faint voice sounded remarkably close, as if she was just on the other side.

"I'm right here, sugar. I'm pulling out the nails. But you have to get off the door or you'll fall through, and I won't be able to catch you."

He heard scraping noises above him, then silence.

"Rachel, are you off the door now?"

When her voice came, it was faint. "You have to go. The fire…"

"You think I'm going to leave you up there alone?"

"It was Paul. Paul did this. I think he did everything."

"That's right, we know who it is now, so it's going to be okay. We'll get him, and then you'll be safe."

"You must hate me."

He smiled at the plaintive tone. "Never."

"I didn't listen to you."

"Yeah, you did," he said, his voice coming out in a soft

grunt as he struggled with a particularly difficult nail. "I told you I was trouble, and you listened. Smart girl."

"I didn't believe you—"

"I know. It's okay."

"No!" Her voice rose a little, her obvious fear tempered with frustration. "Listen to me. I didn't believe… you did it."

His fingers faltered on the hammer, nearly dropping it. "You didn't?"

"I know you. Who you are when you're not being a defensive jackass."

A helpless smile curved his lips. "You do, do you?"

She didn't answer.

His gut tightened, and he attacked the final nails with fierce determination, so focused that he didn't realize until the ladder dropped to open the trapdoor that the fire had finally breached the closet door, the crackling flames waiting for him as he dropped. Fire snapped at his pant legs and singed his shoes as he scrambled up the ladder and into the attic.

Rachel lay on her side a few feet away, her eyes closed and her breathing labored. Her face was sooty from the smoke rising through the rough slat flooring into the attic. He crouched beside her, his heart pounding.

Her pale eyes flickered open, and her soot-stained mouth curved into a weak smile. "I knew you were a hero."

He cradled her smudged face. "Yeah, well, we can debate that later. Right now, we're going to get you out of here. Okay?" He helped her to her feet and crossed to the open window, praying Delilah had come through.

She was standing below on the flagstone patio, locking the extension ladder into position. Struggling with the unwieldy contraption, she positioned it against the wall beneath the attic window. It didn't reach the windowsill, ending about five feet beneath.

Damn it. Seth gazed at the gap between himself and freedom.

"You'll have to climb down to it," Delilah called. "I've seen you monkey your way up a fir tree. You can do it!"

He could do it, but what about Rachel? She'd have to climb out of that window into nothing but her trust in his ability to keep her from falling.

Could she do that?

"Rachel?"

Her eyes fluttered up to meet his, her pupils dark and wide. "What?"

"I have to go out the window to the ladder."

She shook her head fiercely. "No ladder."

"We have to go out this way. The closet below is already on fire."

Her chin lifted. "Then you have to go without me."

"No," he said firmly. "We live together or we die together. Your choice. But I'm not going out there without you."

Chapter Seventeen

"Please, Seth. I can't do it." Panic sizzled in Rachel's veins, driving out anything but fear, as black and deadly as the smoke filling the room at her back. "You go. Now."

His hands closed around her face, forcing her to look up at him. His face was soot-smudged and dripping sweat, but in his clear green eyes she saw a blaze of emotion that sucked the air right out of her aching lungs.

"I will not go without you." Each word rang with fierce resolve. His hands clutched her more tightly in place, as if he planned to drag her out the window with him, whatever the consequences.

"Okay." She peeled his hands from her face and gave him a little push toward the window. "Be careful!" she added with a rush of panic as he hauled himself onto the windowsill.

He disappeared over the side, only his fingers on the windowsill remaining in sight. After a harrowing moment, his face appeared over the sill again. "Okay, sugar. Your turn."

Terror gripped her gut, and she almost turned around and ran toward the trapdoor, preferring to take her chance with the fire. But his hand snaked over the side, grabbing her wrist as if he'd read the panic in her expression.

"You can do this. I braved the fire. You brave the heights."

Fly, baby. You can fly. Her mother's voice rang in her ears, a fierce, mean whisper of madness.

No. I won't fly.

I'll climb down like a sane person.

She closed her eyes a moment, mentally working her way through the next few seconds. She'd get settled on the windowsill, get her balance. Seth would be just below. He wouldn't let her fall.

He'd never let her fall.

She swung one trembling leg over the windowsill, clinging to the frame until she was straddling it, more or less balanced. But her imagination failed her. She couldn't visualize a way to get her other leg over the sill without plunging out the window.

"Take my hands, Rachel." Seth's voice gathered the scattered threads of her unraveling sense and tied them together. "Just take my hands and swing your leg over the edge."

She caught his hands. Fierce strength seemed to flow through his fingers into hers, and she swung her leg out of the window. She was hunched in an uncomfortable position, but she maintained her balance.

"This is the hardest point. Get this right, and we're home free." Seth released one of her hands and braced his against the wall. "I want you to slide off the ledge and onto my arm, turning around to face the wall as you do it. Okay?"

She stared at him. "That's your plan?"

He grinned up at her. "Take it or leave it."

She realized, in that scary, crazy moment, that she was helplessly in love with Seth Hammond. Faults and all. Any fire-phobic man who'd haul a drugged, acrophobic basket case out of a burning house was a man in a million. Whatever had driven him in his sin-laden past, he was a hell of a man in the present.

And if he thought he was going to talk her out of what she was feeling, then he had one hell of a surprise coming to him.

"Remember what we did this afternoon?" she asked, sliding her butt off the sill and into the curve of his arm.

His green eyes snapped up to meet hers. "Yes," he answered warily.

She slid the rest of the way into his grasp, anchoring her fingers on the ladder rungs. The hard heat of his body behind her felt like solid ground.

"As soon as I sober up, we're doing that again. Understood?"

She felt his body shake lightly behind her as laughter whispered in her ear. "Understood."

Step by careful step, they reached the safety of the patio together just as the fire trucks pulled into the driveway.

"THERE'S NOT MUCH to salvage, I'm afraid." Delilah kept her voice low as she crossed to where Seth sat next to Rachel's hospital bed. The E.R. doctor had insisted she stay overnight for observation, given how much smoke she'd inhaled. But he was optimistic that she'd be fine in a day or two.

"I know she'll hate losing the mementos of her family," he murmured, brushing his thumb against the back of her hand where it lay loosely in his palm. "But I don't think she'll miss that damned attic."

"You're right about that." Rachel's voice, thick with sleep, drew his attention back to the bed. Her eyes fluttered open. "So, we lived, huh?"

He squeezed her hands. "Yes, we did."

She rubbed her reddened eyes. "I feel like I swallowed a smokestack."

"You nearly did."

The door of the hospital room opened, and Rafe Hunter breezed into the room on the sheer force of his personality, his wife, Janeane, bringing up the rear. Rafe nudged Seth aside and grabbed his niece's hands. "Rachel, darling, are you all right?"

Rachel gave Seth a quick look over her uncle's shoulder.

"I'll be back in a little while," he promised her, backing out of the room to let her family have time with her. Delilah came with him, laying her hand on his arm as he started to slump against the wall.

"There's a waiting room down at the end of the hall," she said, hooking her arm through his. "Ivy and Sutton need to talk to you."

Seth didn't like the bleak tone of Delilah's voice. "What's going on?" he asked as she led him into the small waiting area at the end of the corridor.

Inside were a handful of hospital visitors scattered among the rows of chairs and benches. At the far end, near the big picture window looking out on the eastern side of Maryville, Sutton Calhoun and Ivy Hawkins had their heads together with a grim-looking Antoine Parsons.

All three turned when he and Delilah walked up. "What's happened?" Seth asked, his gut tight with dread.

"Paul Bailey is dead."

Seth stared at Antoine. "I thought you caught him and took him into custody."

"We did. We booked him, and he was waiting in his cell for his lawyer. The guard near his cell had to go referee a fight between a couple of drunks down the hall, and, when he got back, Bailey was dead."

"Murdered?"

"We're not sure." Antoine sounded apologetic. "We don't know if he ingested something or what. The coroner's got the body already and should have the autopsy done in a few days."

"He didn't do all of this by himself," Seth said firmly. "Someone was pulling his strings."

"That's what we think, too," Ivy assured him. "This case isn't over."

Seth ran his hand over his jaw, his palm rasping over the day's growth of beard. "Is Rachel still in danger?"

"Probably not," Sutton said gently. "Paul Bailey was clearly the link. If he was in charge of the company, then whoever had control of him had access to the trucks. Without him, there's no entry point. Whoever did this will just look for another fool to manipulate."

"So the man behind the curtain just gets away with five murders and weeks of tormenting Rachel?" Rage burned in Seth's gut, as hot and destructive as the fire that had licked at his heels in Rachel's house.

"He won't get away with it if we don't let him," Delilah said. "I've been thinking about what you told us. About Adam Brand."

There was an odd tone to his sister's voice that he hadn't heard before. A vulnerability that she'd never really shown, not even as a girl. He looked at her and saw anxiety shining in her dark eyes.

"What about him?" he asked.

"I've been trying to reach him, going around the obvious channels. I called some people we both knew back in the day. And that story about his being on vacation? It's bull. It's just the official story, at least for now."

"What's the real story?" Sutton asked curiously.

Delilah's expression went stony. "The real story is that he's gone AWOL. And the FBI is investigating him for espionage."

Seth shook his head firmly. "No way. Not Brand."

His sister's eyes blazed at him. "Something's really wrong, Seth. Because there's no way in hell Adam Brand would do anything to hurt this country. And now I'm wondering if what's going on with him has anything to do with his reason for having you follow Rachel."

"How?" Seth asked, not sure how to connect the two ideas together.

"I don't know," Delilah admitted. "I can't see an obvious connection." Her chin lifted. "But I'm going to find out."

She pulled out her cell phone and walked over to an empty spot on the other side of the room.

Sutton's gaze followed her movement briefly, then turned back to Seth. "I guess we owe you an apology."

Seth shook his head. "Not yet. Let me get a few more years of the straight and narrow under my belt and then maybe you'll owe me."

"You're really out of the life?" Ivy asked, more curious than disbelieving. "I hear it has a way of sucking you right back in."

"I don't want the guilt," he said simply. "It's not a life you can live if you have any sort of conscience, and apparently my daddy didn't blow mine up in that explosion after all."

Sutton looked at him through thoughtful eyes and gave a brief nod. "Good for you, Hammond. Prove everybody wrong."

"Speaking of daddies, you talked to yours recently?" Seth asked.

"I went by to see him once I was back in the country," Sutton answered. "He's getting back a lot more of his functions than I think he ever believed he would."

"I should have insisted he keep up with the therapy," Seth said with regret. "I'm sorry."

"He wasn't ready then. You couldn't have made him." Sutton shrugged. "You went above and beyond. I owe you."

"Not yet," Seth repeated with a faint smile.

He waited a few more minutes, giving Rachel time with her family, until he could stand it no longer. He left the waiting room and headed back down the hall to her room.

Her aunt and uncle had gone, but Rachel was still awake. "Where's the family?" he asked as she smiled sleepily at him.

"I asked them to call Diane," she told him, her smile fading. "To let her know what's going on with Paul."

She didn't know Paul was dead, he realized. He was tempted to keep that information from her until she felt better.

But that wasn't fair, was it? Keeping things from her would only convince her she couldn't trust him. He'd damned near been burned—literally—by his secrets. If he was serious about the straight and narrow, serious about becoming a man who could deserve a woman like Rachel Davenport, he had to start by telling the truth, even when it was unpleasant.

Even when it hurt.

He pulled up a chair by her bed and took her outstretched hand. "I just talked to Ivy and Antoine about Paul."

Her fingers tightened around his. "He's in really bad trouble, isn't he? That's why I wanted Uncle Rafe to talk to Diane. She's always liked him. He'll break it to her gently."

"I don't know how to say this but just say it. Paul is dead."

Her fingers went suddenly limp in his. "Dead? How?"

He told her what he knew. "It's possible he smuggled something into the jail. If we're right about someone pulling his strings, it may be that he found death preferable than whatever his puppet master had in store for him."

"He used to gamble in college—Diane used to bail him out all the time—but he went to rehab for it."

"Sometimes—a lot of the time—good intentions aren't enough. Sometimes, rehab doesn't stick."

Silence fell between them as they each considered the double meaning of his words. Rachel spoke first. "Someone made Paul do this. I don't think he'd have done anything this terrible if he wasn't under extreme pressure."

Seth wasn't as inclined to give Paul Bailey's motives the benefit of the doubt, but he couldn't argue with her logic. "The police are looking into Paul's background, trying to figure out who he owed. If we figure that out, we'll be able to protect you better."

"So you think I'm still in danger?" She sounded deflated.

"Not the way you were, no. We don't think so. Paul was the leverage to get a foothold in the trucking company. Without him, whoever was pulling his strings can't get control over the trucks, and we're pretty sure that's what he wanted."

"You don't have any idea why he wanted control of the trucks?"

"Obviously the idea is to use them to ship some sort of contraband. We just don't know what."

"Couldn't they buy their own trucks?"

"Probably not without greater scrutiny."

"So he might already be under investigation?"

Seth thought about Adam Brand. Had the FBI agent tugged the tail of the wrong tiger? "Probably. We just have to match the suspect to the crime."

"We do?" She quirked an eyebrow at him. "You've joined the Bitterwood P.D. now, hero?"

He smiled at the thought at first, but his smile quickly faded. It was a surprisingly tempting idea, he realized. And if he hadn't burned his reputation to the ground, maybe he'd have had a chance to try his hand at being one of the good guys. "No, but I'm interested in the outcome of the case."

Her lips curved again. "Because of me?"

Helpless to say no, he nodded. "Because of you."

Her smile widened briefly but quickly faded. Tears welled in her eyes, and she brushed them away with an angry swipe of her fingers. "Poor Diane. She's lost everyone."

"She didn't lose you. Right?"

Her fingers tightened around his. "Thanks to you."

He kissed her knuckles. "There were a few minutes there I thought I was going to have to stay in that attic with you until the fire got us."

"I wouldn't have let that happen," she said firmly.

He smiled at her confident tone. "Yeah, you say that now."

"I meant what I said up there."

Heat flushed through him as he remembered what she'd said, but he didn't want to assume they remembered the same thing. She'd been drugged, after all. "Which part?"

Her lopsided smirk reassured him that they *were* thinking of the same thing. "You know which part."

He shook his head. "What am I going to do with you?"

Her smirk grew into a full grin. "You need me to remind you?"

"I'm still a risky bet, Rachel. Not everyone's going to be able to see beyond my past. They're going to think you're crazy for wanting to be with me...."

She pushed herself upright in the bed, leaning toward him to place her hand on his cheek. "I'm a big girl. I can take it. What I can't take is life without you in it."

Gazing into her shining blue eyes, he realized she meant every word she was saying.

He closed his hand over hers where it lay on his cheek. "I'm going to do everything I can to make sure you never regret your decision. I promise."

She leaned closer, brushing her lips against his. "That's a good, solid start. Don't you think?"

He wrapped his arms around her, careful not to get tangled in her IV tube. "Yeah, it is," he growled in her ear, breathing in the smoky sweet smell of her, letting it fill him with hope. "It's a very good start."

* * * * *

COMING NEXT MONTH from Harlequin® Intrigue®
AVAILABLE JULY 23, 2013

#1437 SHARPSHOOTER
Shadow Agents
Cynthia Eden
Sydney Sloan is ready to put her past behind her—only, her past isn't staying dead. She doesn't know if she can trust sexy ex-SEAL sniper Gunner Ortez...or if he is the man she should fear the most.

#1438 SMOKY RIDGE CURSE
Bitterwood P.D.
Paula Graves
When Delilah Hammond's former lover, injured FBI agent Adam Brand, mysteriously lands on her doorstep, she risks everything to help him catch a criminal who'll stop at nothing to destroy Adam's reputation.

#1439 TAKING AIM
Covert Cowboys, Inc.
Elle James
Tortured former FBI agent Zachary Adams must battle his own demons while helping a beautiful trail guide rescue her FBI sister from a dangerous drug cartel.

#1440 RUTHLESS
Corcoran Team
HelenKay Dimon
Paxton Weeks's newest assignment is to keep a close eye on Kelsey Moore. But when Kelsey's brother is kidnapped, Pax is forced to add bodyguard to his list of duties....

#1441 THE ACCUSED
Mystere Parish: Family Inheritance
Jana DeLeon
Alaina LeBeau thought returning to her childhood home would help her reconnect with lost memories, but someone doesn't want her to remember. And the gorgeous town sheriff, Carter Trahan, is determined to find out why.

#1442 FALCON'S RUN
Copper Canyon
Aimée Thurlo
Relentless and hard-edged, Detective Preston Bowman knew that helping ranch owner Abby Langdon solve a murder depended on keeping his emotions in check—but destiny had yet to have its say.

You can find more information on upcoming Harlequin® titles, free excerpts and more at www.Harlequin.com.

HICNM0713

REQUEST YOUR FREE BOOKS!
2 FREE NOVELS PLUS 2 FREE GIFTS!

HARLEQUIN®

INTRIGUE®

BREATHTAKING ROMANTIC SUSPENSE

YES! Please send me 2 FREE Harlequin Intrigue® novels and my 2 FREE gifts (gifts are worth about $10). After receiving them, if I don't wish to receive any more books, I can return the shipping statement marked "cancel." If I don't cancel, I will receive 6 brand-new novels every month and be billed just $4.74 per book in the U.S. or $5.24 per book in Canada. That's a savings of at least 14% off the cover price! It's quite a bargain! Shipping and handling is just 50¢ per book in the U.S. and 75¢ per book in Canada.* I understand that accepting the 2 free books and gifts places me under no obligation to buy anything. I can always return a shipment and cancel at any time. Even if I never buy another book, the two free books and gifts are mine to keep forever.

182/382 HDN F42N

Name _____ (PLEASE PRINT) _____

Address _____ Apt. # _____

City _____ State/Prov. _____ Zip/Postal Code _____

Signature (if under 18, a parent or guardian must sign)

Mail to the Harlequin® Reader Service:
IN U.S.A.: P.O. Box 1867, Buffalo, NY 14240-1867
IN CANADA: P.O. Box 609, Fort Erie, Ontario L2A 5X3
**Are you a subscriber to Harlequin Intrigue books
and want to receive the larger-print edition?
Call 1-800-873-8635 or visit www.ReaderService.com.**

* Terms and prices subject to change without notice. Prices do not include applicable taxes. Sales tax applicable in N.Y. Canadian residents will be charged applicable taxes. Offer not valid in Quebec. This offer is limited to one order per household. Not valid for current subscribers to Harlequin Intrigue books. All orders subject to credit approval. Credit or debit balances in a customer's account(s) may be offset by any other outstanding balance owed by or to the customer. Please allow 4 to 6 weeks for delivery. Offer available while quantities last.

Your Privacy—The Harlequin® Reader Service is committed to protecting your privacy. Our Privacy Policy is available online at www.ReaderService.com or upon request from the Harlequin Reader Service.

We make a portion of our mailing list available to reputable third parties that offer products we believe may interest you. If you prefer that we not exchange your name with third parties, or if you wish to clarify or modify your communication preferences, please visit us at www.ReaderService.com/consumerchoice or write to us at Harlequin Reader Service Preference Service, P.O. Box 9062, Buffalo, NY 14269. Include your complete name and address.

HI13R

*When Jacie Kosart's twin sister needs rescuing from a
dangerous drug cartel, she turns to tortured former FBI
agent Zachary Adams. But can Zach put aside his own
demons to help a beautiful damsel in distress?*

Read on for a sneak peek of
TAKING AIM
by
Elle James

Zach staggered back. The force with which the woman hit
him knocked him back several steps before he could get
his balance. He wrapped his arm around her automatically,
steadying her as her knees buckled and she slipped toward
the floor.

"Please, help me," she sobbed.

"What's wrong?" He scooped her into his arms and carried
her through the open French doors into his bedroom and laid
her on the bed.

Boots clattered on the wooden slats of the porch, and more
came running down the hallway. Two of Hank's security
guards burst into Zach's room through the French doors at the
same time Hank entered from the hallway.

The security guards stood with guns drawn, their black-clad
bodies looking more like ninjas than billionaire bodyguards.

"It's okay, I have everything under control," Zach said.
Though he doubted seriously he had anything under control.
He had no idea who this woman was or what she'd meant by
help me.

Hank burst through the bedroom door, his face drawn in tense lines. "What's going on? I heard the sound of an engine outside and shouting coming from this side of the house." He glanced at Zach's bed and the woman stirring against the comforter. "What do we have here?"

She pushed to a sitting position and blinked up at Zach. "Where am I?"

"You're on the Raging Bull Ranch."

"Oh, dear God." She pushed to the edge of the bed and tried to stand. "I have to get back. They have her. Oh, sweet Jesus, they have Tracie."

Zach slipped an arm around her waist and pulled her to him to keep her from falling flat on her face again. "Where do you have to get back to? And who's Tracie?"

"Tracie's my twin. We were leading a hunting party on the Big Elk. They shot, she fell, now they have her." The woman grabbed Zach's shirt with both fists. "You have to help her."

"You're not making sense. Slow down, take a deep breath and start over."

"We don't have time!" The woman pushed away from Zach and raced for the French doors. "We have to get back before they kill her." She stumbled over a throw rug and hit the hardwood floor on her knees. "I shouldn't have left her." She buried her face in her hands and sobbed.

Zach stared at the woman, a flash of memory anchoring his feet to the floor.

Don't miss the second book in the
COVERT COWBOYS, INC. *series, TAKING AIM by Elle James.*

Available July 23, only from Harlequin Intrigue.

INTRIGUE

HEART-POUNDING ACTION MEETS UNBELIEVABLE PASSION!

Two years ago former SEAL sniper Gunner Ortez saved Sydney Sloan's life on a mission gone wrong. And ever since then, he'd been watching her back. Now a hostage-rescue mission in Peru is about to blow the Elite Ops agents' lives apart once again. As the threats against Sydney escalate—endangering the life of the child she is carrying—Sydney knows Gunner is the only one able to save her again…and is the greatest risk to her heart.

SHARPSHOOTER

BY *USA TODAY* BESTSELLING AUTHOR
CYNTHIA EDEN

Only from Harlequin® Intrigue®.
Available July 23 wherever books are sold.